THE GHOSTWRITER
SECRET

Read all the Brixton Brothers Mysteries:
The Case of the Case of Mistaken Identity
It Happened on a Train

BRIXTON BROTHERS

THE

GHOSTWRITER

SECRET

FoR LANDON!

BY

Mac Barnett

ILLUSTRATIONS BY

Adam Rex

SIMON & SCHUSTER BOOKS FOR YOUNG READERS
New York • London • Toronto • Sydney

SIMON & SCHUSTER BOOKS FOR YOUNG READERS
An imprint of Simon & Schuster Children's Publishing Division
1230 Avenue of the Americas, New York, New York 10020
This book is a work of fiction. Any references to historical events, real people, or real locales are used fictitiously. Other names, characters, places, and incidents are products of the author's imagination, and any resemblance to actual events or locales or persons, living or dead, is entirely coincidental.
Text copyright © 2010 by Mac Barnett
Illustrations copyright © 2010 by Adam Rex
All rights reserved, including the right of reproduction in whole or in part in any form.
SIMON & SCHUSTER BOOKS FOR YOUNG READERS is a trademark of Simon & Schuster, Inc.
For information about special discounts for bulk purchases, please contact Simon & Schuster Special Sales at 1-866-506-1949 or business@simonandschuster.com.
The Simon & Schuster Speakers Bureau can bring authors to your live event.
For more information or to book an event, contact the Simon & Schuster Speakers Bureau at 1-866-248-3049 or visit our website at www.simonspeakers.com.
Also available in a Simon & Schuster Books for Young Readers hardcover edition
Book design by Lizzy Bromley
The text for this book is set in Souvenir.
The illustrations for this book were rendered digitally with a Wacom tablet and Photoshop CS3.
Manufactured in the United States of America
0813 OFF
First Simon & Schuster Books for Young Readers paperback edition October 2011
4 6 8 10 9 7 5 3
The Library of Congress has cataloged the hardcover edition as follows:
Barnett, Mac.
The ghostwriter secret / Mac Barnett ; illustrated by Adam Rex. — 1st ed.
p. cm. — (Brixton Brothers ; 2)
Summary: Twelve-year-old Steve is investigating a diamond heist but the case suddenly changes when the author of the Bailey Brothers detective novels writes him a letter to say that he fears for his life.
ISBN 978-1-4169-7817-6 (hardcover : alk. paper)
[1. Mystery and detective stories. 2. Authors—Fiction. 3. Crime—Fiction.] I. Rex, Adam, ill. II. Title.
PZ7.B26615Gh 2010
[Fic]—dc22
2009052021
ISBN 978-1-4169-7818-3 (pbk)
ISBN 978-1-4424-0956-9 (eBook)

For Paul Saint-Amour, Dan Birkholz,
and David Foster Wallace—three wise men

CONTENTS

CHAPTER		PAGE
I	SUNDAY	1
II	POLICE TROUBLE	7
III	A STRANGE CALL	17
IV	AN ALARM IN THE NIGHT	24
V	A NEW CASE	28
VI	JEWEL HEIST!	31
VII	A SECRET UNCOVERED	37
VIII	UNIDENTIFIED FLYING OBJECT	42
IX	DEATH THREAT	46
X	A MYSTERIOUS LETTER	50
XI	A CALL FOR HELP	52
XII	AN INTERROGATION	55
XIII	SEARCHING FOR CLUES	62
XIV	A SINISTER TRAP	67
XV	SECURITY BREACH!	74
XVI	A TRUE CHUM	76
XVII	THE INVESTIGATION BEGINS	83
XVIII	SPADEWORK	86

Contents

CHAPTER		PAGE
XIX	BREAKING AND ENTERING	91
XX	THE MISSING MAN'S ROOM	96
XXI	A DEADLY MISTAKE	101
XXII	A TERRIBLE STRUGGLE	105
XXIII	CAPTURED!	111
XXIV	UNDERWATER CHAOS	114
XXV	DANGER FROM ABOVE	118
XXVI	THE BEE SYNDICATE	121
XXVII	TWO DETECTIVES	127
XXVIII	THE VIPERS' DEN	135
XXIX	THE BEES' NEST	138
XXX	GHOSTWRITERS	142
XXXI	THE TRAIL GOES FRIGID	145
XXXII	A HUNCH	155
XXXIII	IT HAPPENED AT MIDNIGHT	158
XXXIV	EAVESDROPPING	164
XXXV	FIRESTORM	169
XXXVI	TROUBLE IN THE HOSPITAL	173
XXXVII	GOING HOME	178
XXXVIII	BIG CITY CHASE	183
XXXIX	THE VANISHING SEDAN	188
XL	CAPTURED! AGAIN!	191
XLI	WELCOME NEWS	194
XLII	A DARING PLAN	199
XLIII	AMBUSH	202
XLIV	AN UNDERGROUND ESCAPE	206
XLV	FIENDISHLY BETRAYED	211
XLVI	THROUGH THE FOREST	219
XLII	CASE CLOSED	223

THE GHOSTWRITER
SECRET

CHAPTER I

SUNDAY

·

IT WAS SUNDAY, which was Steve Brixton's least favorite day of the week, and the sun was setting, which was Steve Brixton's least favorite part of a Sunday. But Steve was on his living room couch reading Bailey Brothers #19: *The Strange Case of the Strangest Stranger*, which was part of Steve Brixton's most favorite series of all time: the Bailey Brothers Mysteries.

The Bailey Brothers Mysteries were fifty-eight high-octane adventures featuring Shawn and Kevin Bailey, two quick-thinking, hard-punching teens who never met a case they couldn't crack, a motorcycle they couldn't ride, or an avalanche they couldn't cause and subsequently survive. Sleuthing ran in their family: They were the sons of the great American detective Harris Bailey, and they were terrific sleuths in their own right.

There were fifty-eight thrilling and perfect Bailey Brothers mysteries in all—starting with Bailey Brothers #1: *The Treasure in Trouble Harbor* and ending with Bailey Brothers #58: *Spacejacked!*—all written by the same author, MacArthur Bart.

MacArthur Bart, a.k.a. America's Mystery King, a.k.a. Steve's hero, had also written the book Steve loved above all others: *The Bailey Brothers' Detective Handbook*. The handbook was packed with Real Crime-Solving Tips—stuff like How to Make a Plaster Cast of a Scoundrel's Shoe Print, and Surefire Methods for Defusing Some Kinds of Time Bombs. Basically all the high-level supersleuth stuff.

Steve had the handbook pretty much memorized, but he still carried it around with him wherever he went. In fact Steve had all the plots to the Bailey Brothers Mysteries memorized, but he still liked reading the books second and third times. Plus it was research, since a few weeks ago Steve had officially opened his own business, the Brixton Brothers Detective Agency. Steve didn't have a brother, or even a sister, but putting "brothers" in the name of your detective agency was a great way to make it sound totally ace.

Right now Steve didn't have a case to work on, which was why he was lying on the couch—the living room aglow with the last of the day's sun—and finishing chapter eighteen of his book. A gang of car thieves had just captured the Bailey Brothers and was holding the boys in a sea-cave hideout:

"You creeps will never get away with this!" dark-haired Shawn Bailey hollered. "Crime doesn't pay!"

The large lawbreaker with the salt-and-pepper beard looked up from the game of cards. "It doesn't, eh?" he growled. "Then hows come we've got enough tourin' cars and roadsters stashed away in the old barn to make a fortune?"

Shawn and Kevin exchanged a knowing glance. Now they knew where the lawbreakers were stowing the stolen cars! If only they could get free and notify the police. Behind their backs the brothers redoubled their efforts to undo the knots that bound their hands.

"Gin!" shouted the tattooed crook, slapping his cards on the table. "I win again!"

The bearded hood turned to his fellow criminal and frowned. "Go sit on a stalactite, Charlie."

"I think you mean stalagmite," interrupted Kevin, who had taken honors in geology. "Stalactites grow from the roof, and stalagmites grow from the ground."

"An easy way to remember," Shawn chimed in, "is that the *c* in 'stalactite' stands for 'ceiling,' and the *g* in 'stalagmite' stands for 'ground.'"

"Enough!" roared the bearded lowlife. "I'm gettin' tired of all this jabberin'. Charlie, gag this pair of Goody Two-shoes until Smokestacks Samuels gets back and tells us what to do with them."

The man called Charlie stood up and grinned. Gripping two oily rags in his tattooed hand, he limped over to the corner of the cavern where Shawn and Kevin were kept. "This ought to muffle youse two." He sauntered up to Shawn first and reached for the boy's face.

Just then, Shawn untied the last knot and freed his hands. Quickly, he brought his fist around in a powerful haymaker punch to Charlie's solar plexus! The goon collapsed on the limestone floor.

"You kayoed him, Shawn!" whooped Kevin. "Coach Biltmore would be proud!"

Shawn grinned and removed the knife from Charlie's belt. He hurried over to his brother, making sure to hold the knife with its blade pointing down while he ran, and quickly sawed through Kevin's bonds.

Meanwhile the big bearded baddie was lumbering toward them, holding a blackjack in his left hand. "It's gonna be fun whackin' you two over the head," he snarled.

"One, two, three!" counted Kevin, and at once the two brothers bum-rushed their opponent. The large man flew back against the cavern wall and slumped to the floor, unconscious. "Jumping junipers!" Kevin exclaimed, brushing his blond hair aside. "We sure took care of those two!"

"You bet we did," his younger brother replied. "Now what do you say we tie them up and hide out in this cave? I'll bet you dollars to doorknobs Smokestacks Samuels will be back any minute."

"We can surprise him!" Shawn agreed. "Then we'll learn his real identity!"

"I can't wait to find out who the ringleader of the Viper Gang really is," Kevin remarked.

Suddenly a silhouette appeared on the rocky outcrop near the roof of the cavern. A high, clear voice rang out in the darkness. "You boys will never make it out of here alive. Nobody messes with Smokestacks Samuels!"

Just then, a high, clear voice rang out in the Brixton household. Steve froze.

CHAPTER II

POLICE TROUBLE

"STEVE, DINNER!" He put down his book.

Sunday was Taco Night. Steve hated Taco Night— most of the bright yellow shells were broken before they even got out of the box, and the ones that weren't just snapped in your hand when you tried to load them up. Steve got off the couch and trudged into the dining room.

His mom, Carol Brixton, was already sitting at the table. So was a man with a blond mustache, tan uniform, and shiny badge.

Great. It was Rick.

Rick was Steve's mom's boyfriend and Steve's

Rick wielded his taco like a flick-knife.

number one enemy—after lawbreakers and evil-doers, that is. (And honestly, Steve hoped that one day he would discover that Rick actually was a lawbreaker—then his mom would have to break up with him—although more and more it seemed like he was probably just a doofus.) Rick always came over for dinner on Sundays. One more reason to hate the day.

"Grab a taco," said Steve's mom.

"All right!" said Rick. Rick had already taken the only unbroken taco shell and was now rolling up his right sleeve. There, on his bicep, was a tattoo. "Check it out, Steve. I just got it." The skin on Rick's arm was still a little puffy.

The Bailey Brothers' Detective Handbook has some interesting things to say on the subject of tattoos:

Shawn and Kevin Bailey size up everyone they meet: You never know who might be a villain in disguise! Remember that fable about the wolf in sheep's clothing? Well, sometimes criminals are like wolves, except instead of sheep's clothing they wear the clothing of normal, law-abiding citizens. But even though you can change your outfit, there's one thing you can't

change: tattoos! Almost all criminals have
tattoos, and if you're an expert like the
Bailey Brothers, those tattoos tell you
what kinds of criminals they are. Here
are some common criminal tattoos and
what they mean:

Safecracker

Car Thief

Smuggler

STRUGGLIN'
~ to do some ~
SMUGGLIN'

Smuggler Who
Fakes a Haunted
House to Conceal
His Hideout

Cat Burglar

Forger

Blackmailer

Racketeer or

Hit Man

Corporate Crook

Unfortunately, none of those tattoos matched what Rick had on his arm, which looked like this:

"What is it?" Steve asked.

"It's a dragon speaking the Chinese character for courage," Rick said, like it was the most obvious thing in the world.

Steve squinted at the tattoo. "It looks like the dragon is eating the Chinese character for courage."

Rick frowned. "Well, it's not."

"Okay."

"Have a taco shell," Carol said, and put two pieces of shell on Steve's plate.

"What were you reading in there, Steve?" Rick asked.

"Bailey Brothers."

Rick chuckled, which meant that he was laughing at a joke he was about to make. "Shoulda known. Seems like you're reading more mysteries than you're solving there, detective."

"Well, I've only had a detective agency for a couple of weeks, Rick," Steve said.

"I can't believe you're letting him do this, Carol," Rick said as he shook a spoonful of refried beans toward his taco shell, trying to dislodge the brown mash.

"Oh, come on, Rick," Carol said. "It's just a little hobby."

"It's not a hobby, Mom," Steve said. "It's a profession."

Rick rolled his eyes. "Profession. You think you can be a detective just because you got lucky on that one little job." Rick was referring to Steve's first case, *The Case of the Case of Mistaken Identity*, when Steve had saved the United States of America.

"But Steve," Rick continued, "fighting crime is a job for grown-ups. Well-trained, efficient, intelligent grown-ups. People like me." Rick was grabbing some shredded lettuce from the bowl in the middle of the table. He was using his hand, even though there was a pair of salad tongs right in the bowl. "If you ask me, these Bailey Brothers books are giving you funny ideas. Kid detectives! Ha!" He actually said "Ha!" instead of laughing. Steve clenched his fist and cracked the piece of taco shell in his hand.

"You know," said Rick, stroking his mustache thoughtfully, then putting his hand back in the lettuce bowl. "I should write a book about solving mysteries. I could do a much better job than what's-his-name, Mark Borneo—"

"MacArthur Bart."

"Yeah, him. My book, well, it would be about guys like me. Adult detectives. Police detectives. Guys who solve cases through research and diligence and elbow grease. There wouldn't be any of these ridiculous car chases and explosions."

"That sounds like a really fun book, Rick," said Steve with a straight face. His mom smiled a little.

"It would be fun!" said Rick. "Fun and educational. I'll betcha that Bart guy doesn't know anything about real-life crime."

"You know there are salad tongs, right, Rick?" said Steve.

"Steve!" said Steve's mom. She wasn't smiling anymore.

For a minute the only sound was the crunching of taco shells.

"Alls I'm saying," Rick said, "is that when I was Steve's age, I had normal hobbies, like football and chasing girls." Carol frowned. Rick added, "And I was on the debate team."

Steve found that hard to believe.

Carol took a sip of water. "Maybe you should join the debate team, Steve."

"Great idea," said Rick.

"Except our school doesn't have a debate team," said Steve.

"Start one!" Rick and Carol said at the same time, and then started laughing together.

This was bad, even for a Sunday.

"When I—"

Rick's cell phone went off. His ring tone was a few bars of smooth jazz, repeated over and over again. Steve hated smooth jazz.

Rick let the phone ring for a bit, bobbing his head and grinning. Then he answered it. "Sergeant Elliot here. . . . Hi, Chief. . . . Really? . . . Oh, wow. . . . I'll be there right away. Yeah, yeah, I'm on the case."

He flipped the phone closed and stood up. "Sorry, guys. Gotta go. Big case. Huge. And Chief Clumber wants me to take the lead on it."

"Do you really have to go now?" asked Carol.

"Duty calls," said Rick. He looked at Steve and smiled. "Time to do some of that real detective work I was telling you about," he said, tapping the side of his head. There was a piece of lettuce in his hair.

He gave Carol a kiss and Steve a nod and hurried out the door. Steve's mom was quiet. Now that Rick had left in the middle of dinner, she'd be in a bad mood. You didn't need to be a detective to figure that out.

For the rest of the meal Steve just let his mom vent about her boss at the hospital, and when they were finished eating, Steve cleared the table and did the dishes without his mom having to ask. As he scrubbed a skillet, he thought about Rick out on a big case. He looked down at the pan. Food was burned and stuck to the bottom, and it wasn't coming off. Sundays were awful.

He put the pan in the dish drainer and went upstairs to his crime lab.

CHAPTER III

A STRANGE CALL

THE DOOR TO STEVE'S CRIME LAB, a.k.a. his bedroom, had a piece of Scotch tape that ran for a few inches along its bottom and connected to the jamb. The tape was a security system—if the tape was loose, someone had broken into Steve's room. (Villains were always breaking into the Bailey Brothers' crime lab to scare them off their cases.) Steve checked the tape to see if it was intact. It was.

Two weeks ago, when Steve had decided to open his own detective agency, he had used the hundred dollars his grandma had given him last Christmas and converted half his bedroom (which was not all that large) into a crime lab. He'd modeled it on the Bailey Brothers' headquarters.

Steve Brixton was now the proud owner of the following sleuthing tools:

- One typewriter, missing the *T* key, which was unfortunately needed to type Steve's name. The Brixton family computer worked better, but his mom wouldn't let him keep it in his room. Plus the sound of the keys clacking was pretty ace.
- One metal detector, for finding buried treasure, bought secondhand at the Ocean Park Pawn Shop, which technically was "off-limits" to Steve but only because his mom didn't understand the art of detection.
- One ten-pound bag of plaster of Paris, for casting footprints and tire-tread marks.
- Assorted mustaches (handlebar, biker, one that looked like an old black-and-white movie star's, and another that looked like Mr. Mike's, his PE teacher.)
- A disguise chest containing one sailor suit, one milkman outfit, and one Soviet uniform that was a couple of sizes too big.
- Lots of rope, because you never know when you're going to need some rope.

He'd also budgeted for a Dictaphone, which was a machine that Shawn and Kevin used to record all their crime-solving theories for their mom to type out later. But apparently you couldn't buy a Dictaphone anymore, so Steve spent the rest of his money on Jolly Ranchers. Jolly Ranchers weren't really a detective tool per se, but they were his favorite candy. Well, really, the green Jolly Ranchers were his favorite candy. He'd eaten all those on the first day (his tongue had turned green and slick, and the depressions of his molars had filled to the top with hard apple-flavored sugar). Steve had thrown out all the grapes, because grape was a bad flavor of any candy, always. He'd gotten rid of the blue raspberries, too—they didn't taste that bad, but their neon color made Steve uncomfortable. Nothing in nature was that color. Maybe the water around an electric eel. Certainly not any fruit. Anyway, now Steve had a huge bag of red Jolly Ranchers. And this was a problem. Because his second favorite flavor, watermelon, was red, but so was the flavor he hated most: cherry, a.k.a. disgusting cough syrup. And since watermelon and cherry looked exactly the same, Steve was constantly putting the wrong one in his mouth and then spitting it out. (The name of the flavor was printed on the wrapper in such tiny writing that you pretty much had to use a magnifying glass to read it, and who had one of those handy? Okay, Steve did, but it's not like he had time to launch an investigation every time he wanted a candy.)

And then, of course, in Steve's backpack were the three items indispensable to all detectives—a notebook, flashlight, and magnifying glass—plus his secret book-box, which Steve had made himself by hollowing out the middle of an old copy of the *Guinness Book of World Records*. Steve was all set to solve a mystery, as soon as one presented itself.

In the meantime Steve would do what he had done every Sunday for the last two years: write a letter to

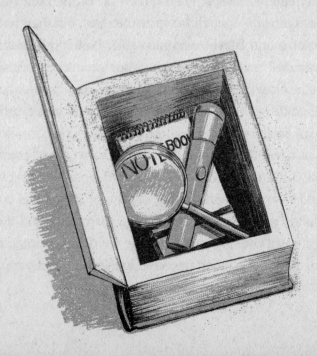

MacArthur Bart, the author of the Bailey Brothers Mysteries. He mailed the letters care of Bart's publisher in New York, but MacArthur Bart never wrote back. The only mail Steve ever got was *Highlights* magazine, which as far as Steve could tell was read only by toddlers and dentists. His grandmother had bought a subscription years ago, and it wouldn't stop coming.

Anyway, Steve didn't hold MacArthur Bart's silence against him. Maybe MacArthur Bart was busy working on a new Bailey Brothers book (it seriously had been decades since the last book had come out). Or maybe the publishing company wasn't forwarding his mail (although Steve had written more than a hundred letters). Whatever the case, MacArthur Bart would definitely have a good reason for not writing back, so Steve had already forgiven him. Besides, how could you be mad at a guy who wrote top-notch stories like *The Strange Case of the Strangest Stranger*?

So Steve sat down at his desk and started typing, leaving spaces to write the *t*'s in later:

```
Dear Mr. Bar ,

I 's me again, S eve Brix on. I hope
you received  he clipping I mailed you
las week from  he Ocean Park Forum. I
```

was abou my new de ec ive agency, and
I men ion you and your books. I don'
have much to repor his week—no cases
or any hing. I guess Ocean Park isn'
as exci ing as Benson Bay—seems like
 he Bailey Bro hers always have a case
 o work on, even hough Benson Bay has
3 de ec ives: Shawn, Kevin, and heir
dad. I guess i has only been a couple
weeks since my firs case. Anyway, I
know I always ask you his, bu are
you ever going o wri e ano her Bailey
Bro hers book?

Rick was over for dinner onigh .
Remember I wro e you abou him? He
said he could wri e a be er de ec ive
book han you. I almos laughed in his
face. He doesn' even

The phone rang. Steve stood to go answer it, but
his mom got to it first.

"Steve, phone!" she yelled from the living room.

"Who is it?" Steve yelled back.

"Don't yell from upstairs, Steve!"

"But you're yelling too!"

"Don't be a smart mouth! Come get this phone!"

He ran down to the living room and took the handset from his mom.

"Is this Mr. Brixton, the detective?" asked a quavering voice on the other end of the line.

"Yes," said Steve.

The man on the phone exhaled. It sounded like a beach on a windy day. He paused. "Mr. Brixton," said the man, "this is Victor Fairview." He said his name like he expected Steve to recognize it, and Steve did. Victor Fairview was the richest man in Ocean Park. "Please come to my estate immediately. I have a case for you."

CHAPTER IV

AN ALARM IN THE NIGHT

THE YELLOW TAPE, hanging at a height of five feet and blocking the winding path up to Victor Fairview's mansion, read, in bold black letters, POLICE LINE: DO NOT CROSS. Steve Brixton, four feet ten inches tall, walked under it without ducking.

"Hey, kid! What do you think you're doing?" shouted an officer, who hurried over to Steve. The officer's police-issue slicker, which kept out the damp from the fog, looked like a cape as he ran. "Can't you read? This is a crime scene. You can't come in here."

Steve, who was wearing shorts and had cold legs, walked over to the officer, reached into his pocket, and pulled out a Velcro wallet. The sound of it ripping open was the only noise in the night. Steve withdrew a card and handed it to the officer:

STEVE
BRIXTON
Private Investigator

the Brixton Brothers
Detective Agency

Fully Licensed and Bonded   (831) 406-1325

The sergeant tensed and his eyes opened wide. "Sorry, Steve. Couldn't tell it was you in the fog and the dark and everything."

"No problem, Officer Johnson." Everyone was impressed with Steve's new business cards. He'd typed them up on the computer and printed them on some heavy paper, then cut each one out by hand. The edges didn't all come out even, but you couldn't tell unless you were looking at more than one of them, and who was ever going to get more than one of Steve's business cards? The part about being "fully licensed" wasn't exactly true—his detective's license had come in the mail after Steve had sent twelve cereal box tops and $1.95 shipping and handling to an address in Kentucky. And the part about being bonded wasn't true at all—Steve didn't even know what "bonded" meant. But it sure looked good on a business card.

"I didn't know you had a brother," said Officer Johnson.

"I don't," said Steve.

"But your card says 'the Brixton Brothers Detective Agency.'"

"Yep."

"So why does it say that if you don't have a brother?"

Steve sighed. "It just sounds cooler."

"Oh," said Officer Johnson. "Right."

They stood quietly for a few seconds in the fog.

"Well, I better get up there," said Steve, nodding toward the main house. He could feel goose bumps popping up on his arms and legs.

"All right," said Officer Johnson with a wave.

Steve was so cold that he wanted to sprint up the path to Fairview's mansion, which was well lit and sure to have central heating. But that wouldn't have looked very detective-like. *The Bailey Brothers' Detective Handbook* says, "Ace sleuths must always keep their cool—even when the danger is red-hot!" And although there was nothing red-hot about the present moment, Steve still didn't want to look like a chump. So he put his hands in his pockets and slowly sauntered up the winding path, clenching his jaw hard so that his teeth wouldn't chatter.

The front door was tall and black, and it had one of those handsome brass lions with a ring in its mouth. Steve rapped three times.

An alarm went off inside the house. Spotlights illuminated the mansion grounds. Steve could hear shouts inside.

CHAPTER V

A NEW CASE

A FEW SECONDS LATER the alarm stopped. The door opened with a creak.

The man who answered the door had a large cordless drill in his gloved hand and a piece of lettuce in his blond hair.

Great. It was Rick.

When Rick saw Steve, he rolled his eyes.

"Terrific," said Rick. "The Great Detective is here."

"Hi, Rick," said Steve.

"Don't you have homework?"

"Finished it." Steve nodded toward the drill. "Did you give up police work and become a handyman?"

Rick's face went cloudy. "What? Oh. This? No. This is a . . . Who called you, anyway?"

"I did." An old man appeared next to Rick. He wore a purple paisley smoking jacket and a scowl. "I don't remember authorizing you to answer my door, Officer . . ."

"Once again, my name's Elliot, Mr. Fairview." Rick straightened. "Sergeant Elliot. I figured since you were busy turning off that alarm again, and since I'm the lead investigator on this case—"

"You figured wrong," Mr. Fairview said, and then turned to Steve. "You looked taller in your newspaper picture."

"Everybody says that," Steve replied.

Fairview nodded. "Come inside. I've just been robbed."

The diamond case had been ransacked!

CHAPTER VI

JEWEL HEIST!

"THIS IS THE DIAMOND ROOM," Mr. Fairview said, waving his hand carelessly around him. "Although now it is without a diamond." Steve's eyes adjusted to the dark. He walked into the middle of a tremendous atrium, and his footfalls echoed. The floor was an alternating pattern of marble squares, black and deep red, like a checkerboard. Steve had never been in a room this big in his life. Or a room this strange. The whole place was empty except for a black pedestal on a red square in the center of the room, illuminated by a powerful spotlight. On top of the pedestal was a clear box with a large hole cut in it. The box held a black pillow, and nothing else.

The room was filled with the sound of Rick's hurried footsteps as he ran up behind them. "I really don't know why he's here, Mr. Fairview. The Ocean Park Police Department has the situation under control. We've secured the crime scene, and there's really nothing left to—"

"Please, Officer . . ."

"Sergeant Elliot."

"Yes. Listen. This is my house. I called the detective here for a reason. I want him on this case. He is now my employee, and my guest, and you will treat him with respect."

Rick's sigh bounced off the Diamond Room's walls.

Mr. Fairview continued. "This pedestal is where I kept the Nichols Diamond, rated by *Billionaire* magazine as one of the top three diamonds in the world."

"I've never heard of *Billionaire* magazine," said Rick.

"Why am I not surprised?" said Mr. Fairview.

Steve hadn't heard of *Billionaire* magazine either, but that didn't keep him from chuckling.

"The diamond is priceless," said Mr. Fairview. "Although if I had to put a price on it, I'd say three hundred and four million dollars."

Steve tried to give a low whistle, but he wasn't a great whistler. So instead he asked, "What does it look like?"

"It is bright red, about an inch long and half as wide. It's the only thing in my house that I really care about. And not just because it's the most expensive, which it is. My wife used to wear it around her neck." Fairview looked past Steve, remembering.

"A red diamond?" Steve asked.

"Red diamonds are the most valuable color of diamond, Steve," Rick said.

"And I believe you learned that fifteen minutes ago, when I told you, Officer," said Mr. Fairview. Steve liked this guy.

"You just left the Nichols Diamond out in the open?" Steve asked.

"I like to look at it. But I was confident the diamond was secure. The diamond has a microscopic chip attached to one of its faces. If it's removed from this room, an alarm sounds, and all the exterior doors and windows lock. The thief will be trapped inside the house. It's a very expensive system. Top of the line."

"Then how did—"

"It didn't work. Earlier tonight, right after I finished my dinner, I heard a noise in the house. I thought it was nothing, but moments later someone came up behind me and put a rag up to my mouth and nose. And everything went dark."

Steve nodded. Chloroform. Baddies were always knocking guys out with chloroform in the Bailey Brothers books.

"The next thing I knew, I was waking up on the rug underneath my dining room table. I called the police. They came right over, and we checked the house for any signs of the robbery. Nothing—until we got to this room. When I discovered the Nichols Diamond was missing, I called you. I don't understand it. The thief must have shorted the alarm. The thing didn't go off until much later, after the police arrived."

Rick smirked. "And then it wouldn't stop," he said. "The thing keeps going on and off, on and off. Old man Fairview keeps having to reset it. It's totally screwy—the robber must have introduced some sort of computer virus or something into the security system. Just shows you, all the technology in the world's no match for the brainpower of a smart crook. But even a smart crook is no match for a good investigator." He knocked the knuckles of his free hand against his skull.

Mr. Fairview stared at Rick for a moment, then resumed. "So what do you say, Steve? Will you take the case? Anything you could do to recover the diamond and bring the thief to justice would be greatly appreciated."

Steve nodded. He took off his backpack, unzipped it, and removed a big brass magnifying glass. Then he started looking around the pedestal for clues. Nothing. He heard Rick snort. Steve took a look at the hole cut into the box. It was perfectly round and big enough to put a hand through. But no fingerprints. Rick chortled. Steve moved on to the floor, examining the marble for hairs, clothing fibers, anything, any kind of clue. Finally Rick spoke.

"Hoo boy! The Great Detective at work. You really think you're in one of those Bailey Brothers books, don't you? Look: You can put away that magnifying glass, Steve. I've already combed the place. And I found a clue as soon as I got here. Didn't need a magnifying glass, either." He raised the drill in his right hand and squeezed the trigger. A high-pitched whir sounded through the room. "The thief forgot his drill," Rick shouted over the noise. He released the trigger. "The idiot left it right by the pedestal. And it's covered with fingerprints. We'll take it back to the station, run the prints through the computer, and we'll know who this guy is in no time. He may have been smart, but Rick Elliot's smarter."

"Can I see that?" Steve asked.

Rick shook his head. "Sorry, Steve. Evidence. I'm not letting this out of my hands."

Rick pretended to draw the drill like an Old West gunslinger and pointed it at Steve.

"He's been carrying it around all evening," said Mr. Fairview. "He seems to enjoy making that noise."

Steve started pacing around the room, keeping to the black squares. His brain worked better when his body was moving. Rick continued talking.

"Sorry, Steve. I'm afraid I've already cracked the case wide open. It's only a matter of time before Rick Elliot gets his man. And the diamond, too, assuming it hasn't been sold."

Steve stopped. "I don't think it's been sold."

"Trust me, Steve," said Rick. "Thieves tend to sell jewels right after they're stolen."

Steve fixed his eyes on Mr. Fairview. "The diamond hasn't been stolen."

CHAPTER VII

A SECRET UNCOVERED

"OH, COME ON," RICK SAID.

"I don't understand," said Mr. Fairview.

"Steve's saying you faked the crime," said Rick, rolling his eyes. "Now he probably wants me to arrest you."

"No," said Steve. "I'm saying the diamond hasn't been stolen. Not yet. Rick has it."

Rick let out an exasperated gasp. "So now I'm the thief! I guess I'm supposed to arrest myself!"

"No," said Steve. "But the diamond's in your hand."

Rick looked at Steve like he was crazy. "This is a drill."

"*Inside* the drill, Rick," said Steve. "It's hidden some-where inside the drill. The thief must have known about the alarm. He knew he couldn't get the diamond out of here, so he figured he'd let the police do it for him. He left the drill, covered with fingerprints—which I'm sure belong to someone else. He was counting on you to take it as evidence. That's why the alarm was going off—you were leaving the room with the diamond. He must have been planning to steal the drill later, from the police station."

Rick scoffed. "How would someone break into the Ocean Park Police Station?"

"Through the bathroom window," said Steve. That's how Steve had done it on his last case. "Or maybe he was just going to rob you on your way back to the station."

"Come on, come on," said Victor Fairview. "Let's have a look at the drill."

Rick put a glove on his other hand and examined the handle. Victor and Steve crowded around him. Sure enough, the bottom of the drill unscrewed to reveal a secret compartment. Inside was a bright red diamond.

"Amazing!" said Mr. Fairview, grabbing the dia-mond and placing it in the pocket of his jacket.

Rick was standing silently on a black square.

Steve smiled. He too was standing on a black square. If this had been a giant game of checkers, Steve could have jumped him.

"I still doubt they would have been able to steal it from the police station," muttered Rick. Fairview arched his eyebrows, but Rick continued. "Anyways, now it's personal. I'll catch the guy who did this."

"How?" asked Fairview. "Your only clue just turned out not to be a clue."

"Oh, I'll find a way. Rick Elliot always gets his man."

"You could set up a plant," Steve said.

"What's that?" asked Fairview.

"Well, the thief doesn't know we're onto him. So take the drill back to the station with a decoy diamond in it. And put a tracking device on the decoy. Let the thief take the drill, then follow him to his hideout. That's how the Bailey Brothers tracked down the gang of tomb raiders stealing antiquities in *Fiasco in Cairo*."

"Brilliant!" said Fairview.

"Yeah, we probably would have done something like that anyway," Rick said.

"But what will you use as a decoy?" Fairview asked.

Rick stroked his mustache.

"You could use a red Jolly Rancher," Steve said.

Rick scoffed. "We'll come up with something better than some cherry candy."

"Red could be cherry or watermelon," Steve said. Who thought of gross cherry first? Only Rick.

"Whatever," Rick said. "We're not using hard candy."

Steve shrugged. "Just trying to be helpful."

"Well, if the Ocean Park Police Department needs your help, we'll ask for it."

"Okay," Steve said.

"Steve," said Victor Fairview, "can I speak with you for a moment?"

"Sure," said Steve, and followed Fairview into an adjoining hallway while Rick looked on.

"Steve," said the old man, "I don't feel safe having the diamond in this house until the thief is caught. I know detectives will often protect valuables for a client. Do you have a hiding place where the diamond will be secure?"

Steve didn't even have to think. "Yes," he answered.

Fairview nodded. He pulled the diamond out of his pocket and placed it in Steve's hand. Steve took a closer look at it. It was translucent and glittered marvelously in the light. He took out his backpack and put the diamond in his zippered pencil case for the time being.

"How much do you charge, Steve?" Fairview asked.

"Two hundred dollars a day, plus expenses," said Steve. "Although on weekdays it's seventy-five percent off, since I'm in class most of the time. And for a job like this, which doesn't require any real investigating, I'd be willing to give you a discount, so maybe like—"

Victor Fairview reached into the inside pocket of his jacket and handed Steve a single green bill. When Steve looked down at it, he thought it was counterfeit money. He didn't recognize the man in the portrait.

"It's a portrait of Madison," said Mr. Fairview. "Consider it a reward for finding the diamond and some money to get you started."

Steve looked closer. It was a five-thousand-dollar bill.

CHAPTER VIII

UNIDENTIFIED FLYING OBJECT

"HEY, CHUM," said Steve to his best chum, Dana.

"Don't call me chum," said Dana to his best friend, Steve.

It was Monday, one week later, after school. Steve and Dana had met up on the road that wound along the ocean. They walked home with their hands in their pockets, like they always did.

"Do we have any math homework?" Steve asked.

"No—just the worksheet that we finished in class."

They watched a pelican swoop low and skim, open-mouthed, along the water.

"Did you know Dana Powers's parents got her her own phone line?" Dana asked.

"Yeah," said Steve.

Dana Powers was a girl in their class. When their new teacher, Mr. Meyer, had shuffled the seating plan last week, her desk was moved next to Dana's, which was completely confusing. Whenever their teacher called on Dana, both of them would start talking at once, and everyone in the class would laugh.

Now Dana talked about her every day.

"I wish I had my own line," Dana said.

"Why? I'm the only person who calls you."

"Yeah."

"You just wish you had Dana Powers's phone number," Steve said.

"Yeah," said Dana, grinning.

The pelican, its mouth drooping, flew upward.

Steve hesitated before speaking again. "Don't you think it would be weird if your girlfriend's name was Dana?" he asked.

"Why?" Dana replied, too quickly.

Steve shrugged.

Dana looked at the ground.

The boys walked a little further.

"Well," Steve said, "aren't you going to ask me how my case is going?"

"No," said Dana.

Dana was what Steve called a "silent partner" in the Brixton Brothers Detective Agency. Being a silent partner meant that Dana didn't carry a business card, that his name didn't appear on the company letterhead, and that he wanted nothing to do with the Brixton Brothers Detective Agency.

Dana sighed. "How's your case going?"

"Not great." Steve shook his head. "Chief Clumber called me this morning to say the fingerprints on the drill didn't match anything in their database. I expected that, since the drill was just a decoy. After school I told the nurse I needed to call my mom, but I called the police station instead to see if anyone had taken the drill. They hadn't. But that's all right—the thief's probably waiting for the case to get cold and the police to lose interest. And even then, he'll probably break in at night."

Dana nodded, but Steve could tell he wasn't really paying attention.

Steve stopped in front a blue mailbox and took an envelope out of his backpack. It was his letter to MacArthur Bart. Steve paused and rubbed the envelope against his chin. "I wrote Bart about my case,"

Steve said. "Maybe now he'll write back. Although it's not like guarding a diamond is as exciting as a Bailey Brothers adventure."

Dana frowned. "Steve, maybe being a detective isn't always like the Bailey Brothers books."

Steve felt the skin on the back of his neck get tight. "What do you mean?"

"Just that in real life, being a detective might not always be big clues and danger at every turn and stuff."

Just then, something whizzed past Steve's head, missing his temple by inches and hitting the mailbox with a large clang. Dana dropped to the ground and yanked Steve down with him. They both lay like snakes with their bellies on the road while more stones rained down from above.

Steve covered his head with his arms. "We're under attack! Someone's trying to kill us!"

CHAPTER IX

DEATH THREAT

A BARRAGE OF ROCKS HIT THE GROUND, throwing up dust all around Steve. He crossed his fingers on one hand and used the other to dig *The Bailey Brothers' Detective Handbook* from his backpack. He opened it to a section called "Falling Rocks!"

When rocks fall from the sky, it can only mean one thing: rock slide! Every detective runs into a landslide or two on the job, so the Bailey Brothers are experts at avoiding them. You can be too! When rocks fall from above, it's

a good bet the ground underneath you
is about to slide away. But Shawn and
Kevin have a nifty trick to avoid going
splat—if you're swept over a cliff, all
you need to do is grab on to a tree or
sturdy weed and hang there until help
arrives! Oh, and one more thing: Don't
get walloped on the noggin by a boulder.

Steve was pretty sure this wasn't a landslide, since
they were on a flat stretch of land next to a beach, but
he grabbed a dandelion patch with his left hand, just
in case. He used his right hand to place the handbook
on top of his head, and just in time, too. A stone rico-
cheted off the shiny red cover and bounced on the
ground.

"Are you crazy?" Dana shouted. "You almost hit
him on the head!"

Suddenly the rocks stopped flying. Dana and
Steve stood up and brushed the dust off their shorts,
squinting in the direction of the attack. A bulky form
emerged from behind one of the cardboard trash cans
that lined the beach road.

It was Nate Rangle.

Nate Rangle had transferred into the seventh grade
three years ago, and he'd stayed there ever since.

Nate's greasy hair hung over his eyes, and his arms hung at his sides like giant sunburned sausages. As he walked up to Steve and Dana, they could see that he was grinning. His braces gleamed in the sun.

"Well, if it isn't Sherlock and Watkins," said Nate.

"Watson," said Steve.

"Shut up," said Nate, and Steve did, but only because he didn't have anything else to say.

Dana was angry. "What's your problem, Nate?"

"You. You guys were in the way of my rocks."

The three boys stood on the road by the water. Steve and Dana glared and Nate smirked. The wind blew lightly. Then, suddenly, Nate lunged forward. Steve flinched, but Nate just bent down and snatched Steve's envelope from the ground. He'd dropped it in the commotion.

"What's this?"

"It's a letter, Nate. Give it back. I dropped it."

"I think I'll keep it." Nate put it in his back pocket. "The Case of the Disappearing Letter. Think you can solve it, detective?" Nate took a step toward them.

"Shut up, Nate," Steve said. He thought about throwing a Shawn Brixton haymaker punch into Nate's solar plexus but figured it would be easier just to rewrite the letter when he got home, especially since he didn't know where Nate's solar plexus was.

Nate pulled a fake yawn. "Hey, Steve, why don't you and your girlfriend get going?"

Steve looked at his chum.

"I'm not a girl," Dana said quietly.

"What?" asked Nate.

"I'm not a girl."

"Then why do you have a girl's name?" said Nate, except he didn't quite finish the word "name," because Dana had punched him in the jaw.

Steve and Dana ran hard. Years of living with a girl's name, or at least a name that girls had too, meant that Dana had learned to punch hard and run fast. Years of being friends with Dana meant that Steve knew when to get a head start. But Nate didn't chase them. He just screamed, "You're dead, Dana Villalon!" And he meant it.

CHAPTER X

A MYSTERIOUS LETTER

ONE WEEK PASSED without much incident. Dana faked a bad flu to avoid facing Nate at school. Whenever Nate saw Steve in the hallway, he ignored him, but Steve figured that meant that Nate was just planning something big, probably waiting till Dana came back. Nobody had tried to steal the drill from the police station yet, and Steve was getting bored waiting. He wished his new case were more exciting.

When Steve got home from school on Monday, his mom was getting ready to leave. On Mondays she worked the night shift at the hospital.

Steve's mom grabbed her tote bag and opened

the front door. "Bye," she said. Then she turned back around. "Oh. I almost forgot. You've got some mail up on your bed."

By the time the front door closed, Steve was already running upstairs. He swung around the corner and into his room. There on his pillow was a copy of *Highlights* magazine. He slumped his shoulders and picked it up. Underneath was a letter.

CHAPTER XI

A CALL FOR HELP

Dear Steve,

First, I must apologize for not having
written you. I'm afraid I am not in the habit
of corresponding with my readers. But I did
receive your letters. And I enjoyed reading
them all, and the article you sent a couple
of weeks ago from your local newspaper.
Well! A real-life Bailey Brother!

Now I must confess to you that I write
under distressing circumstances. I am
currently in Ocean Park, staying at the

Sea Spray Waterfront Hotel. Steve, I have recently received threats that lead me to believe that my life is in danger. I have come to Ocean Park because I am hoping I can hire you. Steve, I need your help.

I would have come in person to your home, but I have reason to believe that I have been followed to Ocean Park, and I would hate to lead the criminals to your family (you and I both know what kind of trouble this can lead to--I'm sure you remember the trained gorilla that broke into the Bailey home in Bailey Brothers #12: The Big Top Caper). Moreover, I fear it may be dangerous for me to appear in public. There is a mailbox around the corner from the hotel. I will post this letter and return to my room. Please come meet me as soon as you receive this letter. I am staying under the name of A. C. Snuffley.

Most gratefully,

MacArthur Bart

MacArthur Bart

Steve grabbed his notebook, magnifying glass, flashlight, and the rest of his detective kit and tossed them all in his backpack. He ran downstairs and wrote a note telling his mom he had gone to Dana's. (Steve figured she wouldn't like it if he was going off to meet some stranger. Of course, this was no stranger—this was MacArthur Bart.)

Steve slammed the front door, ran to the side of his house, and hopped on his bike. He was going to meet his hero.

CHAPTER XII

AN INTERROGATION

THE SEA SPRAY WATERFRONT HOTEL overlooked a quiet beach. Its roof was red and its walls were so white that Steve squinted as he walked up to the entrance. Far away, seabirds whined, and somewhere nearby a leaf blower droned.

What did MacArthur Bart look like? Steve had never seen a picture of him. Would he have glasses? Would he be funny, or very serious? Maybe his hair would be blond, like Steve's. No, it would have to be white, or gray—MacArthur Bart must be pretty old. The Bailey Brothers books were written back in the fifties.

A bored and burly doorman saw Steve hurrying up the path and opened the big glass door. His old-fashioned suit was deep maroon and at least three sizes too small, so it made him look like the rhesus monkey that danced for tourists down on the board-walk. When the doorman's arm was outstretched, his sleeve rode up and revealed a string of tiny letters tat-tooed on his forearm. Steve's eyes snapped on the marking—it was his detective's instinct—and made out the words "rage will always be my last refuge" before the doorman quickly pulled down his sleeve. "Have a good afternoon, Mr. Brixton," he said, rais-ing his little hat.

"How did you—," Steve started, but then caught himself. A good sleuth is never caught by surprise. Steve made a deduction instead. "Let me guess. You've seen my picture in the papers."

"No—I saw it on your backpack."

Right. His name was indeed written in permanent marker, in his mom's handwriting, on his backpack's green fabric. At the beginning of the year she'd written his name on all his stuff—on his water bottle, on his binder, on the tags of all his clothes—so he wouldn't lose them. Steve exhaled through his nose and turned the corner into the lobby.

The dark wood of the lobby floor had a waxy

"Rage will always be my last refuge."

shine. It was the kind of floor that would be fun to slide across in socks. A huge window looked out on a deck with white wicker furniture, and past that, the Pacific Ocean. The place was quiet—Ocean Park's hotels didn't get busy till summer. Smooth jazz played softly from speakers you couldn't see, but Steve was so excited as he walked up to the reception desk that he was only a little irritated by the music.

The man behind the counter had a wispy mustache and glazed eyes. Steve knew from his name tag that his name was Lewis.

"Can I help you?" he asked after Steve had been standing there for a few seconds.

"Yes. I'm here to see A. C. Snuffley. Can you tell me his room number?"

"No," said the man behind the counter. Steve had seen something flash in his eyes when he'd said Snuffley's name.

"Why not?" Steve asked.

"We don't give out guests' room numbers."

"Well, could you call him and let him know Steve Brixton is in the lobby?"

"No," said the man behind the counter.

"Why not?" asked Steve, clenching his teeth and baring them a little, too.

"Who do you think you are? Do you really think

I'm just going to give out private information to some kid off the street?"

"I'm not just some kid." Steve held the clerk's gaze while he removed his detective's license from his wallet and slid it across the table. The man picked it up like it was an old sardine and gave it a cursory glance. Then his eyes widened.

"A detective . . . ," he murmured.

"That's right," said Steve. "Steve Brixton, of the Brixton Brothers Detective Agency."

"The Brixton Brothers Detective Agency," Lewis repeated quietly. Then his eyes snapped back to Steve's. "Where's your brother?"

Steve sighed. "I don't have one."

"What?"

"I'm an only child."

"Then why are you called—"

"You know, it's like the Bailey Brothers."

"The Bailey Brothers?"

"Look, the point is I'm a detective, okay?"

The clerk looked surprised by Steve's ferocity. "Okay." He flung Steve's card back across the counter. Then he said, almost to himself, "I knew that guy was trouble."

"What guy?"

"The guy you asked for, Snuffley."

"What about him?" Steve asked.

"He's had a DO NOT DISTURB sign hung on his door ever since he got here. Weird, but, hey, a lot of these rich folks are strange. But apparently he told room service to bring him the same thing—a bowl of caviar, a plate of smoked salmon, and a cheese platter— three times a day as long as he was staying here, and to leave it outside the door."

Steve felt a twinge of disappointment. There was one difference between him and MacArthur Bart. Steve hated fish—the way they tasted, the way they smelled, and the cold, accusing way they looked at you, even when they were dead and on a bed of ice in the supermarket.

"So here's where things get really odd. Yesterday he didn't eat his lunch. It was just sitting in the hall-way, untouched. Same with his dinner. And today his breakfast and lunch just sat there, too. I've been calling his room, but nobody's answering. I don't know if the guy's died in there or what."

Steve clenched his teeth.

"This Snuffley was very clear that nobody was to bother him about anything while he was staying at the hotel. But if this keeps up tomorrow, the manager says she's opening that door, DO NOT DISTURB sign or no. She wants to find out what's going on in that room. We don't want any trouble here. But now I've got a detective playing twenty questions. And where there's detectives, there's trouble."

Steve could hear his own heartbeat. The letter from MacArthur Bart was dated yesterday. Bart had gone to mail it and never come back.

Steve was too late.

"Where's the nearest mailbox?" Steve asked.

"Around the corner, on Sunset Court. Why?"

Steve didn't reply. He was running for the door.

CHAPTER XIII

SEARCHING FOR CLUES

STEVE PUSHED THROUGH the glass door himself—the doorman was gone now—and it swung open fast and banged against a metal doorstop. He sprinted down the driveway and turned the corner onto Sunset Court, then paused and surveyed the street. Brightly colored houses lined the quiet alley, which ran one block and ended at the beach. There, next to a dented sign about beach safety, was a blue mailbox.

Steve organized the events in his head. MacArthur Bart had left his hotel room, put Steve's letter in that mailbox, and never come back. Which meant that whoever was following Bart must have kidnapped him on this very street. Which meant that Steve was looking at a crime scene. And this time Rick wasn't around to screw everything up.

The Bailey Brothers' Detective Handbook has some useful tips regarding evidence collection:

"Leaping leapfrogs! I've found a clue!" is Shawn and Kevin Bailey's favorite thing to say. That's because clues are Shawn and Kevin Bailey's favorite things to find! When you get to a crime scene, it's super important to walk carefully from one end to another, searching for anything out of the ordinary. You know, clues! Here are common clues that can crack a case:

—Guns or knives
—Hats made in foreign countries
—Gorilla masks
—False beards, wigs, and other fake hair
—Arrowheads
—Anchors and other nautical paraphernalia
—Cryptic notes

—Exotic birds, such as parrots
—Broken swords
—Mesoamerican statues
—Fingerprints, fingerprints, fingerprints!

Steve, walking slowly along the road saw:

—Sand
—Leaves
—An orange peel, shrunken and stiff
—A dirty green visor that said BEACH DUDE

It wasn't impossible that the visor was a clue, but it looked too gross to touch. Steve took out his notebook.

MYSTERY:
WHO KIDNAPPED MACARTHUR BART?

SUSPECT	MOTIVE
Beach Dude?	???
Rick	Jerk

Steve sighed. His suspect list was pretty thin. Fingerprint time.

To know which objects to dust for fingerprints, you had to be able to visualize the crime. Steve saw it happening this way: MacArthur Bart deposited the letter in the mailbox. As soon as the swinging door creaked shut, a black car pulled up, and a thug— perhaps multiple thugs—tumbled out. They came up behind Bart and maybe even put a rag dipped in chloroform up to his face. But there was almost certainly a struggle—MacArthur Bart wouldn't give up without a fight—and it was possible that one of the kidnappers left his fingerprints on the mailbox, probably to steady himself after Bart had punched him in the solar plexus.

Steve crouched down in front of the mailbox and put on a pair of rubber dishwashing gloves. Then he took out a tin of hot chocolate mix and an old makeup brush, dipped the brush in the cocoa powder, and started dusting from the bottom up.

As Steve worked his way up the front of the mailbox, more and more fingerprints began to appear. He kneeled and dusted the handle and door of the mailbox, then pulled the door open so he could dust the other side.

Steve heard a noise from above.

He looked up just in time to see the net drop on him from the second-story window.

CHAPTER XIV

A SINISTER TRAP

THE BAILEY BROTHERS' DETECTIVE HANDBOOK says, "When villains spring a trap on you, it's time to act fast! Don't wait around to see what happens next. Move, move, move!"

But Steve was finding it hard to move, because he was underneath a net. In fact Steve was so astonished to find himself under a net, when just two seconds ago he had been dusting a mailbox for fingerprints on an apparently net-free street near the beach, that he was having trouble doing much of anything.

The net was wet and slimy and smelled terrible. Steve knew that smell. He hated that smell. It was

Steve was caught in a net!

the smell of fish. This was a fishing net. A horrible ripple started in his stomach and worked its way up his throat. Whenever Steve was nauseated, his mom told him to take deep breaths, but now every breath he took brought with it the foul smell of fish. It was terrible, and soon things got worse.

A shiny black sedan screeched around a corner and hurtled toward Steve.

Anyone who's read a Bailey Brothers book knows shiny black sedans are bad news.

The car's headlights flashed.

It was daytime, so the flashing headlights weren't as terrifying as they could have been, but still, the car was going fast, fast enough to jump the curb and run Steve over.

Instead the sedan pulled next to Steve and parked.

A shiny black driver-side door flew open, and a thick-necked man with a shiny black ponytail sprang from it.

Steve tried to run, tripped on the net, and fell to the ground. He thought he heard the bruiser in the black shirt laugh. Steve's face felt hot as he writhed on the ground, struggling to get out from under the net. As he fought to free himself, Steve realized that that was exactly what fish did. Fish didn't just acknowledge that they were caught and stop swimming. They flopped and squirmed and fought for their lives. The ones that were small enough swam through the spaces between the ropes. The rest rubbed and strained against the ropes, maybe making it halfway through a hole before getting stuck. The smell of the net was the smell of their struggle, of the scales and flesh fish left behind in their futile attempts to escape. Steve's stomach twisted. His neck tensed and his head shook involuntarily. But still he tried to get free.

It was no use. The ponytailed brute reached Steve and swept him up, net and all, under one arm. The goon carried Steve back toward the sedan. Steve screamed. He turned his head frantically, to see if anyone was around to help. There was no one on the street. No one on the beach. But he did notice a small tattoo poking out from underneath his abductor's sleeve. It said "rage will always be my last refuge."

This guy must be in cahoots with the doorman!

They were almost to the car. Steve's abductor heaved his arm a bit to adjust the weight of the load he was carrying. A piece of the net went into Steve's mouth. It tasted salty and awful, and Steve thought again of the fish eyes and scales and bits that were on the net and were now in his mouth.

And then Steve threw up.

Steve threw up all over himself and the net and

the shirt of the creep who was carrying him.

The ponytailed man cursed and dropped Steve on the sidewalk.

Steve hit the ground and rolled away from the goon's shiny black shoes. He rolled over once, then again, then stopped when he realized his right arm was free. Everything from Steve's right elbow up was outside the net, and the ocean breeze felt cool on the skin of his forearm. As quickly as he could, Steve lifted his arm and squirmed his way out from beneath the ropes. He scrambled to his feet and took off running.

Steve heard the man shout behind him and looked back to see him, a couple of feet away, his shirt halfway off, stumbling in pursuit.

It's hard to run right after throwing up. Steve was already out of breath and could feel the first twinges of a stitch in his side—but he kept sprinting down the sidewalk. He checked over his shoulder again. The man, now shirtless, was halfway down the block, but had just decided to head back to his car. Steve reached the intersection at the end of the street and turned right onto Pacific Avenue. He paused next to a parked Oldsmobile, put his hands on his knees, breathed deeply, dry-heaved a couple times, and collected his thoughts. Now that he'd turned the corner, Steve felt safe—until he heard tires squeal.

There was no way he could outrun a car.

In seconds the car would turn the corner.

Steve felt sick to his stomach.

Instinctively, Steve threw himself to the ground and rolled under the Oldsmobile. He could feel the pebbles under his back as he looked up at the car's chassis. He heard a car peel around the corner, and turned his head toward the street. He saw the tires of the black sedan speed past him.

Steve waited.

A few minutes later he heard a car driving slowly back toward him. It was the black sedan. The car drove to the end of the block. Then it turned and drove by him again.

The sound of the car's engine grew faint and disappeared. Steve lay flat, breathing hard. He checked his calculator watch: 4:55. He would wait there on his back for a half hour. You couldn't be too safe.

Steve could hear his heart speeding along.

Something smelled terrible underneath this car.

Steve realized it was him.

After a while Steve's legs began to tingle and twitch. Sometimes cars drove past, but the street was mostly still. A man walked by, talking to himself. He was wearing a sandal on one foot and nothing on the other. He stopped by the car for a minute, then moved on.

After a long period of silence Steve checked his watch again. Time: 5:18. Close enough. He rolled out from underneath the car.

The coast was clear.

Whoever had kidnapped MacArthur Bart had just tried to kidnap Steve Brixton, but they had failed.

Steve was onto something huge. Right now, he was the only person who knew MacArthur Bart was missing. He was Bart's only hope. It was time to investigate.

Steve ran toward his house. Halfway home he got tired and stopped running and sped along at more of a quick walk, but when he was a couple of blocks away he started running again.

He burst into his house and leapt up the stairs to his room.

But Steve stopped cold in front of the door to his room.

The piece of Scotch tape on his door was flopping loosely, anchored only to the jamb.

Someone had broken into his crime lab.

CHAPTER XV

SECURITY BREACH!

STEVE RAN TO HIS MOM'S ROOM and grabbed a brass statue of a mermaid from her dresser. The intruders could still be inside his crime lab. Holding the mermaid aloft in his right hand, Steve slowly turned his doorknob. Then, swiftly, he kicked the door open and jumped into his room.

Nobody was there, but the place was trashed. The bag of plaster of Paris was slit open, and a layer of white powder covered almost everything in the room. His sheets had been stripped from his bed and put in a pile along with all his disguises and the clothes from his bureau. The handle of the metal detector was bent at an ugly angle. His mustaches were strewn around the room. Someone was trying to send him a message.

There was a piece of paper in Steve's typewriter. Steve stepped carefully across the bedroom and looked at it:

STEVE BRIXTON: STAY OFF THE BART CASE

Steve smiled. Did these guys really think he could be discouraged that easily? Clearly these hoodlums had underestimated Steve Brixton. Steve practiced the Bailey Brothers' method of detection—Shawn and Kevin's crime lab had been vandalized plenty of times, but that never stopped them. It only made them sleuth harder.

Steve was in danger. A kidnapping ring was after him, and they knew where he lived. But Steve wasn't afraid. He was thrilled. This was a real case.

Steve started pacing around the room, trying not to step on any of his stuff, sorting out the afternoon's events. He wasn't safe at home, and his mom wouldn't be safe while he was in the house. He wouldn't be safe at school, either. Plus he needed every minute of the day to work on this case. Steve stopped walking and smiled. He had a plan.

CHAPTER XVI

A TRUE CHUM

"A FISHING NET?"

It was almost nine p.m., and Steve was at Dana's house, in the kitchen. (Steve was allowed to come over and stay late when his mom was working nights.)

"I know. It was awful."

"Are you sure someone didn't just drop the fishing net out of the building accidentally?"

"And then a sedan just happened to pull up? Driven by a kidnapper with the same tattoo as the doorman who saw my name on my backpack? Come on, Dana. It's like Harris Bailey always says: Coincidences are the lazy detective's crutch."

"What does that even mean?"

"It means there are no coincidences. 'Coincidence' is just an excuse not to investigate something!"

"And which Bailey Brother is Harris? The blond one?"

"He's their dad!"

"Whatever. I still don't think real criminals would use a fishing net."

"What are you even talking about? So many criminals use fishing nets as weapons. Fishnet Johnny is the main henchman in *One, Two, Riddle My Clue*, and he uses a fishing net exclusively!"

Dana sighed.

"And then when I got home," Steve said, "someone had torn up my crime lab. They're trying to scare me off the case."

"I hope it worked."

"Danger is the snack food of a true sleuth."

Dana shook his head. "Is that from Harris Bailey?"

Steve smiled. "Nope. That's from Steve Brixton."

Steve unwrapped a Jolly Rancher and put it in his mouth. He spit it out immediately.

"Hey!" said Dana. "What's the deal?"

"Cherry," said Steve.

"Oh." Dana made a face. "Still, you didn't have to spit it on my counter."

"I was aiming for the sink."

"Well, throw it away or something."

Steve picked up the candy between his thumb and forefinger and tossed it in the trash. Then he walked around the counter and sat next to his friend. It was time to put his plan into action.

"Anyway," he said, "enough about me. Any word from Nate?" Steve asked.

"No," said Dana. "Did you know Nate's dad collects knives?"

"Yikes," said Steve.

"I never should have punched him. I can't believe I have to go back to school tomorrow."

"You don't," said Steve.

"No, I've been faking sick for seven days. I think my dad's onto me. He said—"

Steve pulled a piece of paper out of his pocket and unfolded it. "I just talked to your dad."

Steve triumphantly slapped the paper down on the kitchen counter.

Dear Mr. and Mrs. Villalon,

Great news! As a member of the Ocean Park Middle School debate team, your child is invited to participate in the 37th Annual California Debate

Championship Tournament in San Diego! OPMS will
be competing in this event for the first time, thanks
to Steve Brixton's leadership and initiative in putting
together a team. The tournament starts tomorrow
and continues through the weekend. (We apologize
for the short notice, but Ocean Park's team was just
founded this week, and we only learned this morning
that our late-entry form had been accepted.)

PLEASE NOTE: THIS TRIP WILL BE SUPERVISED
AT ALL TIMES BY RESPONSIBLE ADULTS.

If you have any questions, please contact Principal
Strelow at 432-8544.

----------cut at dotted line----------

Parent Signature _Lorenzo Villalon_

Steve saw Dana was done reading. "A man has
been kidnapped. The clock is ticking. Every hour is
valuable. We won't have time to go to school—we
need to investigate."

"My dad signed this?" Dana asked.

"Yep. So did my mom. I just took it by the hospital."

"But we don't even have a debate team."

Steve smiled.

"This is crazy," Dana said. "I can't believe our parents believed this."

"Are you kidding? Parents love it when their kids join the debate team. People always believe lies if they want them to be true—that's just a fact." This wasn't in *The Bailey Brothers' Detective Handbook*, but that didn't mean it wasn't right on.

"Well, what if they call Principal Strelow?"

"Remember how you wanted Dana Powers's phone number?"

"Yeah."

Steve pointed at the flyer. "Well I got it. I went by her house and gave her fifteen dollars to change her voice mail. Now it just says, 'Thank you for calling. Please leave me a message at the tone.' Very professional. She isn't going to answer calls from numbers she doesn't recognize."

"But what about school?"

"I paid Dana Powers another five dollars to pretend to be our moms and call in sick for us."

Dana groaned. "I don't believe this."

"She's pretty good at voices. Who knew?"

Dana just sat there. It was time to put the pressure on.

"Look," said Steve, "this is an emergency. MacArthur Bart needs our help."

"Why don't you call the police?"

"So Chief Clumber can put Rick on the case? Please. MacArthur Bart didn't go to the cops. He came to me."

"But you're supposed to be on the Fairview case."

"All I have to do is protect his diamond. And I've got that hidden somewhere safe."

"I don't know . . ."

"If you join the investigation, it'll buy you a couple more days to let Nate cool off." Steve extended his hand. Dana stared at it.

"Look, Dana, you need to ask yourself: Do you want to be a Bailey Brother or an Ernest Plumly?"

"I don't even know what that means."

"Ernest Plumly is the Bailey Brothers' stout chum. He's kind of a wet blanket and he's always getting kidnapped."

Dana glared. He'd gotten kidnapped on Steve's last adventure, and apparently it was still a sore subject with him. "I don't want to be a Bailey Brother or an Ernest Plumly. I want to be a Dana Villalon, and I want to have a bowl of cereal and then go to sleep."

"So an Ernest Plumly, then," Steve said under his breath. Then he added, "Dana, the people I'm looking for are dangerous. I'll need a friend out there."

Dana shook Steve's hand.

Steve smiled. "Welcome to the Brixton Brothers Detective Agency, chum!"

CHAPTER XVII

THE INVESTIGATION BEGINS

THE BAILEY BROTHERS' DETECTIVE HANDBOOK tells gumshoes how to start an investigation off right:

You can't fight crime on an empty stomach! If Shawn and Kevin are heading out to do fieldwork, their mom always packs them a nourishing picnic lunch! (And she always packs extra for the Baileys' chubby chum, Ernest Plumly.) Their basket's packed with turkey sandwiches, coleslaw, two pies (one apple, one banana cream), a batch of cookies, a few generous

slices of chocolate cake, and a Thermos full
of fresh lemonade. You know, brain food!

Steve's mom had stopped packing his lunch in the
fifth grade, and anyway, this morning she was still
asleep, so Steve dumped a whole box of Fruit Roll-
Ups and four pudding cups into his backpack.

He ran up to his room and grabbed his notebook,
magnifying glass, flashlight, and the *Guinness Book
of World Records*. Right now the secret compartment
held a bunch of secret stuff, including one thousand
dollars cash, a fifth of the money Fairview had given
him on Sunday. (The rest was in a business savings
account at the Ocean Park Credit Union.) He put
everything in his backpack. Then he took a black permanent marker and crossed out the name his mom
had written on the green fabric—he couldn't have
"Steve Brixton" written on his stuff if he was going
undercover. He put on his pack and tightened the
straps.

Steve was ready to start sleuthing.

Dana knocked on the front door at seven forty-five.
"Where do we start?" he asked.

"The Bailey Brothers always say, 'Start with a little
spadework.'"

"I have no idea what that means."

"You know, digging up everything we can about the missing person. Friends, enemies, connections with criminal gangs or foreign countries unfriendly to the United States."

"But we don't know anyone who even knows MacArthur Bart."

"That's why we have to break into MacArthur Bart's hotel room," Steve said. "Come inside. We need to put on our disguises."

CHAPTER XVIII

SPADEWORK

THE BAILEY BROTHERS' DETECTIVE HANDBOOK says:

The key to sneaking around where you don't belong is to act like you actually belong there. Think of developing a convincing backstory! For instance, in Bailey Brothers #14: *The Secret Behind the Fun House Mirror*, when Shawn Bailey goes undercover as a carnie, he makes up an appropriate nickname (Rock Salt) and invents a story about why he wears a beard (to cover a scar from a tragic bumper car accident). When he tells his tale to gangs at the state fair, they accept him as one of their own!

"Keep it natural," Steve whispered to Dana as he pushed the door open at the Sea Spray Waterfront Hotel. Steve and Dana were dressed as resort guests: They were wearing Hawaiian shirts and brightly colored board shorts. Steve had a camera around his neck (the camera didn't work, but nobody needed to know that). Dana had a straw hat on his head and a beach ball under his arm. "I'll take the lead," Steve whispered. The two boys sauntered up to the front desk. Steve wanted to whistle a carefree tune but settled for humming instead.

The woman working today had a bright pink face and a brass name tag that said LINDA, MANAGER.

"Good morning," she said pleasantly.

"Good morning, Linda," said Steve. "I'm Sam and this is Otis. We're brothers, out here on a trip with our dad. We checked in yesterday, with Lewis, I believe."

"Okay . . . ," said Linda.

"Boy, we're sure enjoying this California weather," said Steve. "It's a different world in Ohio, where we're from."

The manager nodded slowly.

"Tell me," Steve said. "Do you guys have a door-man working at the hotel?"

"No," said Linda. "Why?"

Just like he'd suspected! But there was no time to celebrate his discovery—he had to keep up his identity. "Just curious," said Steve. "When our dad took us on another vacation to Hawaii we stayed at a hotel with a doorman."

"Oh," said Linda. "All right."

Dana spoke up. "When we went to Hawaii, we visited Maui." Nice! Dana was deep undercover.

"Well," said Steve, "we'd better get to our room. Our dad's waiting for us. He's an engineer on the railroad, so he expects everyone to be punctual."

"Sounds good," said the manager.

Steve and Dana walked past the desk and turned the corner into a long hallway lined with doors.

"That was perfect!" said Steve. "Our story was airtight."

Steve and Dana high-fived.

Just then, a pale old couple wearing huge wrap-around sunglasses came walking in the opposite direction. Steve and Dana smiled and kept walking.

"How will we know which room is Bart's?" Dana asked.

"I've thought of that," said Steve. "Yesterday the

guy at the front told me that MacArthur Bart has been ordering caviar, salmon, and cheese for every meal. But since he's been kidnapped, the food's been sitting outside his room."

Steve stopped next to a silver plate, covered with a silver dome, that was sitting on the carpet in the hall. "All we have to do is find the plate that has Bart's meal, and we've got it. Voilà!" He bent down and whisked the shiny cover off the plate. Underneath were a few nibbled pizza crusts, a bowl of soggy lettuce, two dirty champagne flutes, and an empty green bottle.

"That's disgusting," Dana said.

"Yeah."

Steve and Dana strolled down the hotel's nearly endless corridors, peeking under covers at the platters underneath. They found half a croissant; a piece of French toast, soggy with syrup; the bones of some sort of fish (which made Steve gag violently); a glass smeared red with cocktail sauce and holding two white shrimp; pieces of eggshell and a tiny silver pedestal; a single asparagus shoot that looked like a fat-knuckled finger in brown sauce; a vegetal mash that smelled like gorgonzola cheese; a bunch of grapes and a sausage patty; and a plate of six Kobe beef sliders, cold but untouched. They climbed a flight of concrete stairs up to the second floor, walked nonchalantly past a maid and her cart, and continued down another a hallway. There, on the only tray in the corridor, they discovered a bowl of glistening black caviar, a pink fillet of salmon, and a plate of pale and fragrant cheeses.

"We're here!" said Steve.

Dana popped a piece of cheese into his mouth. "That's good," he said, chewing. "How are we going to get inside?"

CHAPTER XIX

BREAKING AND ENTERING

THE BAILEY BROTHERS' DETECTIVE HANDBOOK has a useful chapter called "Picking Locks":

> Picking locks is a breeze! It's also sometimes against the law! But if your heart is good and your intentions are noble, like Shawn and Kevin's, you've got nothing to worry about. Just:

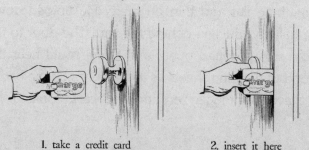

1. take a credit card   2. insert it here

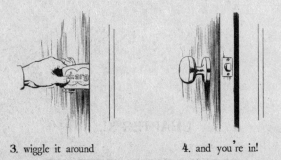

3. wiggle it around   4. and you're in!

Steve took out his Velcro wallet, opened it as quietly as he could (which was not very quietly), and took out his detective's license. It was a little bit flimsy.

"Do you have a credit card?" Steve asked Dana.

"Seriously?" asked Dana.

"Wait here," said Steve.

He sprinted softly back down the hall, his footsteps muffled by the carpet's deep pile. When he got to the end, he froze, got down on the ground, and peered around the corner (it's always best to be above or below eye level when you're sneaking around).

There, twenty feet down the hallway, was the maid's cart, parked outside a room. Maybe there was something flat and thin on there. He tiptoed down the hall and ducked behind the cart. The door to the room was propped open, and Steve could hear the sound of flapping sheets as the maid made the bed.

Steve rummaged around the cart, looking for

something he could pick a lock with. A toothbrush handle would be too thick. The needle from a sewing kit wouldn't be thick enough. He put a bottle of lavender bubble bath in his pocket, but not because it would help him break into Bart's room—it was a gift for his mom.

From inside the room came the soft thudding of pillows being fluffed. Steve didn't have much time. He snuck around to the front of the cart, where, next to a set of keys and a half-full bottle of Diet Coke, sat a white plastic card with "Sea Spray Waterfront Hotel" written on it in cursive. Steve couldn't believe his luck. He slipped the card in his pocket—just as the maid walked out of the room with an armful of bed linens. She stopped suddenly and eyed Steve suspiciously.

"Can I help you?" she asked.

"Oh, I, uh, was looking for an extra washcloth."

The maid smiled, but not warmly, and took a washcloth off her cart. "Here," she said, her hand outstretched. "Next time just ask. Things go missing off these carts."

Steve nodded quickly and hurried down the hall.

When he turned the corner, Dana was lifting a spoonful of caviar to his mouth.

"How is it?" Steve asked.

"Salty," said Dana. "But good."

"You know those are fish eggs, right?"

"Delicious fish eggs."

Steve shook his head. "Look what I found." He reached into his pocket, removed the card, and flashed it in front of Dana's face.

Steve kneeled down with the handbook opened next to him on the floor and slid the card into the crack between the door and the jamb, just above the lock, then started wiggling the card back and forth.

Nothing happened.

"Why isn't this working?" Steve muttered to himself.

"Where'd you get that card?" Dana asked through a mouthful of caviar.

"I took it off the maid's cart."

"But, Steve—"

"I know, I know. It's stealing. But my heart is good and my intentions are noble!" He sawed away at the card.

"Steve—"

"The handbook says it will work. I just need to keep wiggling." The card warped and bent and almost broke, but still nothing happened.

"Steve, stop!" Dana whispered fiercely.

Steve stopped.

"That's the maid's key card," said Dana. "It opens all the doors in the hotel."

"Hey, not everyone gets to go on a trip with their parents every summer and stay in hotels with fancy key cards," Steve said.

"Key cards aren't really that fancy."

"Whatever. I have a lock to pick."

Steve was still for a few seconds, then he slowly withdrew the card. Right in front of his face, next to the handle, was a brass card slot with three little lights on it. He put the card in the slot and quickly removed it. A green light flashed and a lock clicked. Steve tried the handle. The door opened.

"We're in!" said Steve.

Dana smoothed the divot he'd made in the caviar, wiped the spoon on his shorts and put it back on the tray, and replaced the silver dome. Steve took a deep breath. The boys walked through the door, unsure what they'd find on the other side.

CHAPTER XX

THE MISSING MAN'S ROOM

THE CURTAINS WERE DRAWN and glowed at their edges. Otherwise the room was dark.

"My mom says that's the sign of a nice hotel room—when the curtains block out the light even in the daytime. MacArthur Bart's got nice taste," Dana said.

"Of course he does," said Steve. "He's the greatest writer of all time."

Usually Dana rolled his eyes when Steve said that, which annoyed Steve and usually led to an argument. If Dana rolled his eyes this time, it was too dark to see.

Steve walked over to the drapes, yanked them

open, and let the late-morning sunlight fill the room.

Everything was neat and tidy. Steve had half expected upended furniture and dresser drawers strewn across the floor. Instead there was a typewriter on a desk and an empty suitcase on the floor. Three suits hung in the closet: one blue, one tan, one brown. There were socks in one drawer, underwear in another.

Dana dropped his beach ball and took off his hat and backpack. Steve put the camera down on the dresser.

"Look for anything that might tell us something about Bart's disappearance," Steve said. "A letter from someone, a plane ticket to South America, a personal check for a large amount of money. Or a business card," Steve added. "We don't even know where MacArthur Bart lives."

Dana was peering under the bed, using Steve's flashlight. "I think there's a battery under here," he said.

That wasn't very exciting.

"Never mind. It's just roll of mints."

That was even less exciting.

"Actually, it's antacids."

This search was going poorly.

They searched everywhere—every drawer, every

suit pocket, every hard-to-reach corner—for some kind of clue that would tell them anything about what had happened to MacArthur Bart. When they were done, they searched again.

Nothing.

Steve sat down on the edge of the bed. Dana offered him an antacid. He ate it. Then he sighed.

"We don't know anything more about MacArthur Bart now than we did this morning."

Dana was looking out the window. "They have a nice pool here. Maybe we should go swimming."

It wasn't a bad idea—the Bailey Brothers often stopped sleuthing to take a dip—and Steve was about to agree when he noticed a small white notepad on the bedside table. He'd seen it earlier, but—of course!— how had he forgotten? Steve stood up suddenly.

"Dana, give me a pencil."

Dana reached into his backpack and hurried over with a bright yellow pencil in his hand. Steve snatched it from him and sat back down. The Bailey Brothers had used this trick to crack two different cases—*The Symbol of the Wheezing Jaguar* and *The Mystery of the Third Twin*. Now it was Steve's turn. He grabbed the pencil sideways in his fist and rubbed it back and forth against the page.

Dana was peering over Steve's shoulder. "What are you doing?"

"If MacArthur Bart wrote something on this pad of paper, his pen would have left grooves on the next sheet. This is an old detective's trick to reveal what he wrote."

There, in the middle of a cloud of gray, emerged a string of white numbers.

"What is it?"

"Part of a phone number. Probably the last number MacArthur Bart called. This could be a big lead."

"That's the area code for San Francisco. My grand-parents used to live there," said Dana.

"San Francisco . . . ," said Steve, chewing on his thumbnail.

His thoughts were interrupted by the sound of loud footsteps coming up the hall and stopping outside the door. Steve and Dana froze and listened hard. There was some rustling, and then the sound of a key card being inserted in the lock. Someone was coming inside!

CHAPTER XXI

A DEADLY MISTAKE

STEVE AND DANA RAN TO THE BATHROOM and softly shut the door. Three seconds more and they would have been discovered. Steve heard two men enter the hotel room and begin to talk. Their voices were deep and muffled, and Steve couldn't make out a word they were saying. But he knew a baddie when he heard one, and these were definitely two baddies.

Moving slowly, deliberately, silently, Steve picked up a glass from the bathroom counter—two were sitting upside down on little paper doilies—and he nodded at Dana to do the same. Steve placed the mouth of the glass against the door and the conversation in the other room became audible. Dana copied him.

". . . hate stakeouts."

"It's part of the job, Henry. It's part of the job."

Henry! One guy's name was Henry.

"They have a nice pool here. Maybe we should go swimming."

"Wrong. The boss says we're supposed to wait here for that Brixton kid."

Steve's eyes widened. Dana's did too.

"How do we know he's going to come here?"

"The boss was sure he'd show up."

"Great. So we wait. All I'm saying is this is not why I joined up with the Bee Syndicate."

The Bee Syndicate! These must be the kidnappers. Steve wanted to write this stuff down, but he was afraid getting his notebook out would make too much noise. The guy named Henry kept talking.

"Hey," said Henry. "Is that your backpack?"

Steve looked over at Dana. He was not wearing his backpack. Dana apologized with his eyes.

Suddenly the men in the other room got very quiet.

Steve pressed his ear hard against the glass in his hand, straining to hear anything. There was silence, and then, suddenly, the sound of a closet door being opened very fast. They were searching the room. Steve knew where they would look next. There was

Steve and Dana eavesdropped on the two brutes.

only one other place someone could hide, and he and Dana were hiding in it.

Steve scanned the bathroom for something he could use as a weapon. All he could see were towels. Lots of towels. Towels in shapes and sizes he didn't even recognize. Varieties of towel extending far beyond the Big Three of hand towel, bath towel, and washcloth. Who could possibly use all these towels?

Steve reached into his pocket.

The door flew open.

CHAPTER XXII

A TERRIBLE STRUGGLE

STEVE PULLED OUT the bottle of lavender bubble bath, uncapped it quickly, and aimed it at the goon's eyes. He squeezed. Time slowed.

Steve watched the purple fluid flying from the bottle toward the goon's stubbly face; the liquid's arc dropping sharply, way too early; the bubble bath hitting the goon's white shirt with a lavender splatter; the goon's mouth twisting as he laughed a laugh both angry and amused; the plastic bottle falling from Steve's hand and clattering weakly on the bathroom floor.

The man stepped forward, wiggled his fingers, and

closed them into a fist. "So you wanna fight dirty," he said, grinning. "That's fine with me."

The man lunged forward. Steve took a quick step back. And then, out of nowhere, Dana was stepping forward, as in toward their attacker, and Steve noticed that Dana was holding the white ceramic lid from the back of the toilet. He swung the toilet's ceramic lid hard and fast into the man's right knee. The big man doubled over and collapsed onto the floor, holding his leg in both hands. Dana dropped the lid, which crashed on the tile, breaking into three or four large pieces and a puff of white powder.

"Ace!" said Steve. Dana smiled, breathless, and ran out of the bathroom with Steve following right behind him.

They probably shouldn't have been surprised to see the second baddie standing there waiting for them. "I'm a little tougher than Henry," he said, smiling mirthlessly.

Steve glared at him, about to spit out a smart retort that he hadn't quite yet thought of, when he suddenly recognized the man before him.

"You're the doorman!"

Steve looked him up and down carefully: He wore his greasy hair pulled back in a ponytail that glistened in the light from the window. The sleeves of his shirt were pulled low and covered his tattoo.

"Good to see you again, Steve Brixton. Who's your friend?"

"This is my associate, Dana."

"I'm not really his associate," said Dana.

"Dana," said the man. "Cute name. I guess you must be the Brixton Sister."

And with that Dana went rushing toward the doorman.

The Shawn Bailey Flying Tackle, deployed with equal enthusiasm against rival schools' quarterbacks and the underworld's burliest creeps, looks like this:

Dana's bum-rush of the doorman looked more like a remote-control car running at high speed into a wall. Dana bounced off the man, who picked him up and held him, wriggling, in a full nelson.

Steve, determined to rescue his best friend and really wishing he had looked up "solar plexus" in his mom's anatomy book this morning, charged forward. He hadn't taken more than two steps when something hit the back of his foot and he went sprawling onto the carpet. Before he could get up, someone pinned his arms behind his back.

"Nice job, Henry," said the doorman.

Steve craned his neck around and saw that Henry had indeed recovered and was holding both Steve's wrists in one meaty hand. Steve kicked his legs wildly and wriggled his wrists, but the struggle was fruitless.

"All right, grab the rope," said the doorman. "Let's tie these two up."

Henry froze, looking sheepish.

"What is it?"

"Um, I think I left the rope in the car."

The doorman gave Henry the kind of irritated look that probably would have been accompanied by an exasperated gesture were he not using both hands to subdue Dana. "You've got to be kidding me."

"Wait!" said Henry. "I've got an idea." He pulled Steve up to his feet and passed him over to the doorman, who now held Steve in one arm and Dana in the other. Henry disappeared into the bathroom and re-emerged moments later with an armful of fluffy white towels. "These'll work," he said cheerfully, and dropped all but a hand towel on the floor.

Henry unfolded the towel and, taking an end in each hand, ripped it into two thin strips. Steve was impressed. Henry then took one of the strips and tied Steve's wrists together behind his back. Steve was still wearing his backpack, so it was extra uncomfortable. When he was finished, Henry quickly bound up Dana's wrists too.

"Works pretty good," he said. Steve had to admit he was right.

"Are you taking us to where you're holding MacArthur Bart?" Steve asked, trying to keep the note of hope out of his voice. He was sure that if they were held in the same place as Bart, the three of them could engineer an escape.

The doorman raised his eyebrows gleefully. "Look at the detective!" he said. "Think you've got everything figured out, do you? Well, I've got some bad news for you both: You're never, ever going to see MacArthur Bart." The doorman's smile disappeared. "Henry, gag 'em."

A pair of washcloths made excellent gags.

"All right," said the doorman. "It's time to get rid of these detectives once and for all."

CHAPTER XXIII

CAPTURED!

JUST THEN there was a knock at the door.

"Mr. Snuffley? This is Linda, the manager? Um, we're a little worried about you in there, seeing as you haven't eaten any of your food or anything? Are you in there, Mr. Snuffley?"

Henry and the doorman looked at each other, panicked. Steve and Dana tried to shout out for help, but the washcloths muffled their cries.

The doorman called out, "Um, hello, Linda! This is Mr. Snuffley! I'm fine."

"Oh, okay, happy to hear it," said Linda. "Have a good day, sir."

Henry and the doorman exhaled simultaneously, relieved.

Steve's hopes plummeted.

But then there was another knock. "Hi, Mr. Snuffley? Sorry to bother you again. I'm just wondering if you mind if I come in for a moment?"

"Why?" said the doorman tersely.

"Well, a maid's key has gone missing on this floor, and we need to recode the lock on your door."

The doorman cursed quietly and whispered to Henry, "Take these two out on the balcony and make sure they don't do anything unwise." Then, louder: "Just a minute, Linda. Let me throw on some clothes."

Henry opened the sliding glass door that led to the balcony and pushed Steve and Dana outside. The doorman pulled the curtain closed.

It was a little cramped out there for three people. Henry was distracted, looking nervously back at the room even though they couldn't hear any of what was going on in there. Soundproof windows: That had to be another sign of a nice hotel room. Steve looked around, hoping some other guests would be on their balconies and see them, but the place was dead quiet. Below them, the pool sparkled—it looked blue and inviting and, from up here at least, close enough to jump into.

The next few things seemed to happen all at once.

Steve looked at Dana, who looked at Steve, who kicked Henry hard in the kneecap. Henry shrieked, and Dana, hands still tied, climbed backward onto the balcony's ledge. He stood up, wobbled, and jumped. And then Steve did the same thing.

CHAPTER XXIV

UNDERWATER CHAOS

ACCORDING TO *THE BAILEY BROTHERS' DETECTIVE HANDBOOK*:

Shawn and Kevin consider themselves experts on jumping out of tall buildings. And do you know their favorite place to land? Not a barge full of soft garbage (Bailey Brothers #7: *The Great Landfill Caper*), or a hay cart (#16: *Danger Flies the Coop*) or even a truck full of pillows (#21: *The Message in the Factory Whistle*). That's right! It's water!

Whether they're taking swan dives off abandoned lighthouses on Benson Bay or the rocky cliffs of Acapulco (in Mexico!), when it comes to a safe and splashy landing, there's no better surface than good old H_2O!

Steve Brixton also considered himself an expert on jumping out of buildings, although he typically ended up injuring himself in the process. But he fell now with confidence, anticipating the cool, chlorinated cushion of pool water below him. He entered the water feet first (Steve couldn't do a swan dive even when his hands weren't tied behind his back), plummeted downward, and came down mightily on the bottom of the pool.

Water may be soft, but a pool's floor is not.

Steve's hands were smashed between his butt and the concrete, and a sharp pain shot from his wrists to his nail beds. Bubbles streamed from his nose.

Air. Steve pressed his legs hard against the bottom and shot upward, bursting from the surface of the water like a breaching whale. He saw Dana a few feet away, doing some awkward kicking stroke with his hands behind his back.

Steve took a deep breath in through his nose, at

the same time sucking in water from the towel in his mouth. The key was not to panic. The water stung his throat. *Just stay calm and don't panic.* He sank back down in the water.

Again to the bottom and back to the top. This time Steve turned and looked up at the balcony from which he'd just jumped. It was empty. A breath and back downward. When Steve sank, he sank fast. Any kind of swimming would be impossible with this backpack. Steve pushed off from the bottom, breathed in deeply, and disappeared underwater again. Up and down, up and down, like he would do when he was a little kid, when he didn't know how to swim and got stranded in the deep end. Slowly, with every trip to the surface, Steve moved closer to the steps on the other side of the pool. Ten feet. Eight feet. At five feet the water was just an inch or two above his head. By four feet he was walking, coughing against the towel in his mouth. He dragged himself out of the pool. Dana was out already, lying flat on his back.

Soaked, fatigued, with hand towels in their mouths, the two boys lay in the sun, the warm cement radiating pleasantly on their backs.

But not for long.

There was a loud crack that Steve instantly recognized as a gun firing. He turned his head and looked at Dana (Steve's heart now beating loud and fast) and saw that Dana was all right—wide-eyed but all right. And now Steve looked up at the block of rooms that lined the pool, and, sure enough, there was the doorman on the balcony with what had to be a pistol in his hand. There was another shot, and Steve heard it ricochet off a metal deck chair. He turned back to his best friend, and the two of them knew what they had to do. They scrambled to their feet, took a running start, and jumped back into the pool.

CHAPTER XXV

DANGER FROM ABOVE

THREE MINUTES AGO, in this very same pool, Steve had been desperate to get his head above water. Now all he wanted to do was get to the bottom and stay there. He blew all the air in his lungs out through his nose and drifted down to the pool's smooth floor. Eyes open and burning, he watched Dana come to rest on a spot nearby. They wriggled their way across the pool's bottom to the edge closest to the building, for cover.

When he was a little kid and taking swim lessons, Steve didn't have a great breaststroke or butterfly, but he was able to stay underwater longer than any kid in the class. Although it was a lot harder to stay submerged when you were already exhausted and a man was shooting from somewhere twenty feet above your head. It had only been a few seconds, and already Steve wanted air.

One terrible thing about being shot at underwater is being able to see the bullets travel toward you. They came screaming through the pool, swirling streams of little white bubbles trailing behind them. These bullets were coming close. A shot—two feet away, maximum. Steve's ears popped, and his chest heaved. A shot, this one even closer. Steve's lungs felt like they were turning inside out. Nearby, Dana sat with his back against the edge of the pool, his black hair swaying to and fro like seaweed. Another shot. Steve's eyeballs felt ready to burst.

And then nothing. Silence. Stillness. Steve's first thought was that it was a trap. His second was that, trap or not, he needed air. He unfurled his legs, kicked off from the bottom, and, as carefully as he could, poked the top half of his head above water. Air rushed through his nostrils and filled his chest. There were no gunshots. There was a police siren, loud and getting louder. The cops must have scared those crooks away. Dana came up next to him. They made their way out of the pool once again. The siren was close. The police would be here any second.

A path ran from the pool past a wing of the hotel and down to the beach. Steve immediately took off toward the sea. Dana didn't follow. Steve stopped and turned around.

Dana gave Steve a look that meant, *What are you doing?*

Steve gave Dana a look that meant, *What are you doing?*

Dana stomped his right foot, which meant, *I'm staying here.*

Steve nodded his head toward the beach and gave Dana a look that meant, *Come on, man, you need to trust me here. We'll lose hours explaining to Chief Clumber why a man was shooting at us. And then lose more time explaining to our parents why we aren't in San Diego at a debate tournament. We can't afford that time, not when MacArthur Bart is being held by those guys, who are obviously homicidal maniacs. Now hurry up.*

Steve wasn't sure all that got through, but when Dana rolled his eyes, he knew his chum had gotten the gist of it. Steve started running. Dana ran too. They sprinted past a sign that read NO HOTEL TOWELS ALLOWED AT THE BEACH and onto a vast stretch of golden sand.

CHAPTER XXVI

THE BEE SYNDICATE

AFTER A LIFEGUARD untied their towels (Steve invented a cover story about a game of cops and robbers, but the lifeguard didn't seem interested), Steve and Dana walked for miles along the beach. They stopped near a rock jetty that jutted into the ocean. Nearby, a teenage couple sometimes looked seaward and sometimes looked at each other but never once looked at Dana and Steve.

Steve and Dana hadn't spoken while they were walking, but now Dana turned to his friend and shouted, "We could have died!"

(Even now, the couple did not look over.)

Steve nodded gravely. "I knew this would get dangerous. But I didn't know how dangerous. Dana, this is big. MacArthur Bart has been kidnapped by the Bee Syndicate."

Dana, who was flushed and angry, paused. "What's the Bee Syndicate?" he asked.

Steve took out *The Bailey Brothers' Detective Handbook*. It was soggy, and the pages turned in chunks. Steve found the entry he was looking for and laid the book down on the sand. "Look," he said to Dana, pointing to the handbook.

Dana crouched down to read a section called "Crime Syndicates—the Methodical Mayhem of Organized Crime."

Shawn and Kevin always say, "One no-goodnik is bad enough, but a gang of them is positively rotten!" Crime syndicates are groups of criminals who have banded together to break as many laws as possible. Syndicates usually have lots of cash (which they often call dough) and tons of burly rascals eager to get in fistfights with detectives. Shawn and Kevin have spent a lot of time busting up crime syndicates, so they know a thing or two about them.

Three Fun Facts about Dangerous Crime Syndicates:

—They're usually headquartered in run-down warehouses, ramshackle cabins, or secret rooms off the back of ethnic restaurants.

—Their favorite crimes include smuggling, counterfeiting, automobile theft, blackmail, kidnapping, and stealing gold from honest miners' claims.

—They always name themselves after a fierce and dangerous animal, like the Rattlesnake Posse, the Hyena Gang, or the Chupacabra Cartel.

"You can stop there," said Steve.

"So we're up against the Bee Syndicate?" asked Dana.

Steve nodded. "That's right."

"That's not the fiercest animal name."

"What are you talking about?" said Steve. "Bees sting people."

"Right, but a bee sting just hurts a little bit."

"Not if you have allergies."

Dana shrugged. "I guess."

Steve knew Dana knew Steve was right.

"I wonder what MacArthur Bart did to make these guys angry," said Dana.

"Maybe," said Steve, "they're holding him for ransom."

"But then wouldn't there be a ransom note?"

"There probably is one, but we don't know about it." Steve started walking. "We don't know who Bart's family or friends are. The only thing we know about him is that he called someone in San Francisco."

Steve was now pacing a figure eight. "Maybe," he said, "MacArthur Bart stumbled upon the Bee Syndicate and was going to bring them to justice."

"MacArthur Bart writes detective stories. That doesn't mean he's a real detective."

"And so that's why he came to me!" Steve made another loop. "He wanted me to bring this gang down."

"Maybe," Dana said.

"Well, the important thing is that a vicious crime syndicate is holding MacArthur Bart, and we need to find their headquarters before it's too late."

"So what do we do next?"

Steve paced faster.

"Look," said Dana, "before you come up with some crazy plan, I just want to say for the record that I don't really want to get shot at, or even run into those guys, ever again."

Steve said nothing. He just kept moving.

"And so," Dana continued, "even though I know you'll disagree, I really think we should just go to the police."

Steve stopped. "You're right," he said.

"I am?"

"Yes. We will go to the police." Steve smiled. "The San Francisco police."

"What?" Dana asked.

Steve had a feeling, a glowing, tennis ball–size orb of certainty right in his gut. And Steve had read enough Bailey Brothers novels to know what this feeling was: It was a hunch.

"Dana," said Steve. "I have a hunch."

"Oh, no," said Dana.

"The last number MacArthur Bart called had a 415 area code. I have a feeling the solution to this case lies in San Francisco."

"But he could have been calling anybody," Dana said.

"No!" said Steve. "I had to rub that notepad with a pencil to get that number. That means it's a clue."

"That's not enough evidence!"

Dana didn't understand. A hunch didn't need

evidence to be true. A hunch was like a two-legged stool that somehow still managed to support a fat man's weight. A hunch was remarkable, even magical.

"Look, Dana," said Steve. "I have a hunch, and a hunch is the most powerful thing a detective can have." Steve was quoting from Bailey Brothers #1, and pretty much every Bailey Brothers after that. "Now, let's follow that hunch!"

CHAPTER XXVII

TWO DETECTIVES

THE BOYS TOOK A BUS that dropped them off in front of a brown brick building by the water in San Francisco. Streetcars, which looked like they belonged to another century—they were orange and green and blue and had rounded edges and bright white letters—crisscrossed on tracks in the middle of the road. Steve, accustomed to the short buildings and open spaces of Ocean Park, could not stop looking up.

Steve realized that this was the first time he'd been away from Ocean Park without his mom. He was free. He and Dana could do whatever they wanted—but all Steve wanted to do was to solve this case.

The sun was setting, and the wind was cold and whipping hard, so Steve took a jacket out of his backpack. Remembering that Dana didn't have his backpack anymore, and so didn't have any extra clothes, he handed the jacket to his friend.

"This is still damp," Dana said. Steve shook his head.

They ate pizza from a stand at the Ferry Building, and Steve bought himself a sweatshirt embroidered with a cable car on it from a vendor on the street.

They were both tired and decided to continue the investigation the next morning. Steve paid cash for a room at a hotel downtown (and had to give the desk clerk an extra fifty bucks to rent the room to a pair of twelve-year-olds). The two boys flopped onto their beds and fell asleep with the TV on.

The next morning Steve got directions to the Central Police Station, and he and Dana headed out. They arrived at a building that looked like a huge box with little slats for windows. Black-and-white police cruisers and SUVs lined the street for blocks.

Steve and Dana walked through the front doors and into a chaotic lobby. Officers, some holding cups of coffee, some holding files or stacks of paper, hurried around while bored-looking men and women sat in plastic chairs. Phones rang everywhere, all at once.

Steve walked up to the desk sergeant and stood on his tiptoes to look a little taller.

"How can I help you, buddy?" the officer asked.

"My name is Steve Brixton, and I'd like to talk to someone who investigates organized crime," said Steve.

"Why? I mean, what is this regarding?"

"The kidnapping of an important figure," said Steve. "It could be a matter of life and death."

For a little while the desk sergeant didn't say anything. Then, "Please sit down. I'll send someone out to see you."

Steve turned and gave Dana a thumbs-up, and they both took a seat.

Ten minutes later they were still sitting there.

"I'm hungry," Dana said. They'd forgotten to eat breakfast.

"Me too," said Steve.

"Is it cool if I go get us some muffins or something while you talk to the police?"

"Yeah," said Steve. Dana headed out the door.

After another five minutes a tall woman came up to the row of chairs. She was dressed in a gray suit, and her hair was pulled back in tight braids.

"Steve Brixton?" she asked.

Steve nodded and shook her hand.

"Detective Stephanie Taylor," she said. "Nice to meet you. Come with me."

Steve rose and followed Detective Taylor through a swinging door, into an elevator, down a long hallway, and into a small office on the station's sixth floor.

Detective Taylor took a seat at her desk, and Steve took a chair on the other side.

"Now," said the detective, taking out a pad and pen. "What's going on?"

"I'd like to see your file on the Bee Syndicate," he said.

"The what?"

"The Bee Syndicate. A crime syndicate I believe is operating out of San Francisco."

For a while Detective Taylor didn't say anything. Then, "You want to tell me a little more about what's going on, Steve?"

"I have reason to believe that MacArthur Bart is being held captive by members of the Bee Syndicate, and that his life is in danger."

"And who is MacArthur Bart?"

Steve was shocked. "MacArthur Bart? The writer? He wrote the Bailey Brothers Mysteries."

"Oh, those old detective stories?"

"Yes! I would think that as a police officer you would have read those."

Detective Taylor laughed. "Nope. They always seemed kind of goofy."

Steve let it go. They were getting off track.

"So," said Detective Taylor. "What is your relation to Mr. Bart?"

"He's my favorite writer."

"Can you describe him for me?"

Steve was silent. "I don't know what he looks like."

"You don't know him?"

"Not personally."

"What makes you think he's in trouble?"

"He wrote me a letter."

"A letter."

"Yes."

"And are you sure the letter's from MacArthur Bart?"

"Who else would it be from?"

"And he said that he'd been kidnapped?"

"No."

"Did he mention the Bee Syndicate?"

"No." Steve didn't want to get into all the stuff about the shoot-out and the running from the Ocean Park Police.

She sighed. "And why would MacArthur Bart write you, Steve?"

"Because I'm a detective."

Detective Taylor put down her pen. "Are you that kid detective who was in the news a few weeks ago?"

Steve nodded.

The police officer looked at Steve for a long time. "So what you're saying is that you got a letter, from a man you've never met, saying that he was in trouble, and that all you have is a hunch that he's being held here in San Francisco by a gang called the Bee Syndicate."

"That's right," said Steve. "So can I see your files?"

"Listen, Steve, let me tell you a few things. We are a police department. It's our job, not a private detective's, to investigate crimes like kidnapping and organized crime. And we don't just open our 'files' for some kid who walks through our front door." Detective Taylor made little finger quotes on the word "files." "We definitely don't open them up for some out-of-town private eye. And finally, and I'm only telling you this because I'm in a good mood today, I have never heard of a criminal outfit called the Bee Syndicate. Which means that they're not operating here in San Francisco."

"That you know of," said Steve.

Detective Taylor sighed. "Yeah, that I know of." Detective Taylor rose. "I'll walk you outside."

Soon Steve was back in the lobby, sitting down next to Dana.

"How'd it go in there?" Dana asked.

"Pretty well," said Steve. "Only I didn't get any information. Detective Taylor wouldn't even check in her files."

"So now how do we find the Bee Syndicate?" Dana asked.

"Well, we've got to get into those files. I'm thinking that we come back this afternoon, and we say that it's Take Your Kids to Work Day, and our dad brought us to work, but now we're lost, so we need to find our dad, and he works in the place where they keep criminal files. Then, once we know where that is, we go and get some police uniforms and fake mustaches, and we—hey, why are you smiling?"

Dana reached into his pocket and pulled out a yellow piece of paper. "I found this in the phone book."

THE B. SYNDICATE
450 ALABAMA ST..........(415) 642 5585

Steve flushed. "But we're looking for the B-E-E Syndicate."

"How do you know? We never saw it written down. Plus the first eight digits of the phone number match."

He had a point.

"Come on," said Steve. "We could have MacArthur Bart freed today!"

CHAPTER XXVIII

THE VIPERS' DEN

THEY TOOK A CAB and had the driver drop them off a block away from the address on Alabama Street. This part of town was all warehouses, so the sidewalks were mostly empty. Steve and Dana started walking. Nearby, a truck rumbled and shuddered as it backed into a loading bay. And then, across the street, there it was: 450 Alabama. It was a huge building with big windows lining the second floor and no windows on the first. The front door was bright red. It was the perfect base for a gang of criminals.

Above the front door was a small plaque that said THE B. SYNDICATE.

"Wow," said Dana. "I'm surprised they advertise the fact they're a crime syndicate."

Steve nodded. "A lot of crime syndicates pay off the police and politicians so they can operate right in the open like this. That means these guys are really powerful, really dangerous."

As he said those last words, Steve's excitement turned to anxiety and dread. They were about to go charging into a crime syndicate's headquarters. He pulled out *The Bailey Brothers' Detective Handbook* and opened it up to a section near the end called "Raiding the Hideout."

Almost every case Shawn and Kevin investigate ends in a spectacular raid! And whether the baddies have guns, knives, or brass knuckles, the Bailey Brothers have something they don't: the element of surprise! By the time the lawbreakers figure out what's happening, they've already been kayoed! So next time you crash a thieves' den or smugglers' cove, make like your favorite detective duo: Go through the front door, charging hard and thinking fast.

"Okay," said Steve. "Here's the plan. We go running through the front door. The gangsters will probably be playing cards or having a wrestling match or something. MacArthur Bart will be tied up somewhere, maybe in a back room. So we split up. You lead the bad guys on a chase around the warehouse—"

"Why me?" Dana asked.

"Because you're faster. I'll go looking for Bart and untie him. Then the two of us will come and find you, and if we have to, we'll punch our way out of there. It'll be easier to fight with Bart's help."

"But I thought you said Bart must be really old."

"That doesn't mean he can't fight."

"Why can't we just call the police?" Dana asked.

"Because the police don't believe me! They aren't interested in this case. And besides, they need warrants and evidence and stuff. We don't. This is a job for private detectives."

Dana nodded.

"Go!" said Steve.

They ran for the big red door.

CHAPTER XXIX

THE BEES' NEST

STEVE HAD A HEAD START and made it to the door first. He kicked it, and it opened fast, with the high-pitched shriek of ungreased hinges. Steve's momentum carried him a few unsteady steps inside. When he caught his balance, he looked around.

He was dumbfounded.

Steve was ready for almost anything, but this was a surprise: In a brightly lit corner of the warehouse, four men sat at four desks, staring at Steve and Dana, their fingers hovering above computer keyboards (except for one of them, who was using a typewriter). Two desks were empty. The rest of the cavernous building

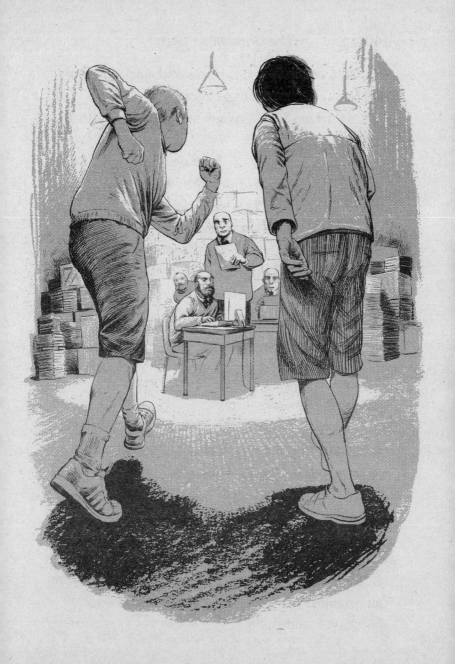

Men worked at desks, wearing bright sweaters and sensible slacks.

was filled with cardboard boxes and stacks of books. Red books. Bailey Brothers books.

"Can I help you?" asked the man closest to the door.

This was not part of the plan. Steve and Dana stepped deeper into the room, and Steve looked closely at the men. They were big men, most of them very hairy, three of them bearded. All of them wore khaki slacks and cable-knit sweaters. Each man's sweater was a different color. One man—the biggest one of them all, a huge, pale man with a bald head and dark black eyebrows—was wearing a sweater whose color could only be described as blue raspberry. None of them looked particularly interested in fighting.

Steve was so confused he couldn't move. What was going on here?

Suddenly a voice came from behind them. "Let me guess: You boys are looking for MacArthur Bart?"

Steve and Dana wheeled around and found themselves looking up at a tall man with a green sweater and a large scar across his face. How had he snuck up on them? The man put a hand on each boy's shoulder. His grip was firm.

"My name is Jack Antrim." He smiled. "What are your names?"

"Dana," said Dana.

Jack Antrim's face brightened. "My mother's name is Dana."

Dana exhaled through his nose.

"And you?" Antrim asked Steve.

"Carl," Steve replied. He was going undercover until he figured out who this guy was and what he'd done with MacArthur Bart.

"Dana, Carl, my office is upstairs. " He nodded toward a set of steel steps, barely visible on the other side of the warehouse, that led up to a mezzanine. "I think the two of you should come with me." He spun them around and squeezed their shoulders so hard it hurt. Steve and Dana walked toward the stairs. They didn't have a choice.

CHAPTER XXX

GHOSTWRITERS

JACK ANTRIM'S OFFICE wasn't even technically a room: only three walls went from the floor to the ceiling, and the fourth wall stopped halfway, so Steve could see the warehouse below and the men typing away. Steve and Dana sat in dingy chairs. Antrim sat behind his desk, which was in front of a large window, so Steve had to squint when he looked at him.

"Dana, Carl." Jack Antrim rubbed his left temple. He paused for an uncomfortable length of time. "You would think after all this time it would get easier, but . . ." He sighed. "This is the hardest part of my job."

This wasn't going at all like Steve expected.

Jack Antrim took a deep breath. "The men down there are all ghostwriters. Do you know what a ghostwriter is?"

"Sure," said Steve. "It's someone who writes ghost stories."

Antrim chuckled gently. "No, but that's a very good guess, Carl. A ghostwriter—"

Steve didn't like Antrim's chuckling, and he didn't like being wrong. So he interrupted. "Then is it someone who writes down things ghosts say?" Steve asked.

"Like a medium," Dana offered helpfully.

"No. Ghostwriters are—"

"You're not trying to tell me that those guys down there are actually ghosts?"

"What? No. It doesn't have anything to do with ghosts, okay? Just listen to me and I'll tell you. Ghostwriters are people who write under different names, instead of their own. Sometimes they write under names of people who exist—for instance, a famous person might hire a ghostwriter to write their autobiography, and then pretend that they wrote it themselves. But sometimes ghostwriters write under the names of people who don't exist at all."

"So what's this got to do with MacArthur Bart?"

"Carl, MacArthur Bart doesn't exist. He never

has. The Bailey Brothers books were written by ghostwriters."

A million questions flooded Steve's skull. It was like his brain was underwater.

CHAPTER XXXI

THE TRAIL GOES FRIGID

"But the sign on the door says you guys are a syndicate!" said Steve. "Doesn't that mean you're criminals?"

Antrim laughed loudly. "You've been reading too many Bailey Brothers books. Yes, we're a syndicate. A literary syndicate."

"What?"

"We're a group of ghostwriters who collaborate on books. The B. stands for Bart—our pseudonym. The original Bailey Brothers books were written by a bunch of different ghostwriters: newspapermen, college students, even a Canadian. You didn't think one man could write fifty-eight books in fifteen years, did you?"

"Fifty-nine," said Steve. "You're forgetting *The Bailey Brothers' Detective Handbook*."

"That's right," said Antrim. His eyes became suddenly sad. "You're obviously a big fan. This must be hard for you."

Steve didn't say anything.

"My grandfather, Ed Antrim, started the B. Syndicate. I guess you could say that he's the real MacArthur Bart, although he died years ago, and he never wrote a single Bailey Brothers book. He hired other people to write them. That way he could publish lots of books very quickly. His writers earned a hundred dollars per book. And my grandfather became a very rich man."

"Why doesn't everyone know about this?"

"A lot of people do," said Antrim. "There are books about it. Magazine articles." He stood and walked over to a large metal filing cabinet. Antrim pulled a key from his pocket, unlocked a drawer and removed a folder, then locked it back up again. "Here, have a look. Of course, most kids who read the books don't know. It would be bad for business. Kids want a hero, someone to believe in. So most adults let kids believe. It's harmless, really."

Steve was looking through the folder. It was true—the first paragraph of almost every article about the B. Syndicate mentioned that MacArthur Bart didn't exist. One magazine article was called "The Man Who Was Never There: MacArthur Bart and the Men Behind the Bailey Brothers Mysteries." Steve was overwhelmed.

"I know this probably wasn't what you were expecting. You were probably hoping to meet your favorite writer today. This happens a couple times a year: A kid will track us down, and then I have to break the bad news to him. We try to keep this address a secret, but I guess MacArthur Bart fans tend to be good detectives." Antrim was looking out the window, but he suddenly turned back toward Steve and Dana. "How did you two find out about us, anyway?"

"What?" said Steve. "Oh. I called the publishers in New York and they gave me the forwarding address." Steve lied without knowing why he was lying.

Antrim frowned. "They're not supposed to do that." He wrote something down on a piece of paper.

"Well, like I said, I'm sorry to disappoint you, boys. But come on," Antrim said, standing up. "The least I can do is give you a little tour."

Steve and Dana followed Antrim back downstairs and onto the warehouse floor. They picked their way around the stacks of Bailey Brothers books.

"Sorry this is such a maze," Antrim said. "We're sort of a combination warehouse and office—it saves on rent."

Steve paused and looked up at stacked copies of *The Riddle of the Eagle's Fang*. That was a classic— the second-to-last Bailey Brothers book ever published. Then Steve thought of something and caught up to Antrim.

"Mr. Antrim, if you guys write the Bailey Brothers Mysteries, and there hasn't been a new Bailey Brothers book in decades, why are you all here?"

"Good question, Carl," Antrim said as they emerged into the open area where the ghostwriters sat at their desks. "We stopped writing Bailey Brothers books years ago, but we'll ghostwrite anything at this point. For instance, the B. Syndicate wrote the Kate Sugarwood, Girl Detective series. You ever read one of those?"

"No," Steve said. They sounded good, but they had pink covers, and Steve was afraid people would laugh at him if he pulled one out at school.

"And we don't just do kid detective series. A lot of books are ghostwritten. Pop stars, presidents, athletes—none of them write their own autobiographies. They hire ghostwriters to do the work for them. Ed over there"—Antrim gestured toward the ghostwriter with the largest beard—"he wrote Cyndi Lauper's memoir."

"Who's that?" Dana asked.

"She wrote that song 'Girls Just Want to Have Fun,'" Antrim said.

"What was the book called?" Steve asked.

"*Girls Just Want to Have Fun*," Ed answered, scratching his beard.

"So why haven't there been any more Bailey Brothers books?" Steve asked.

"Well," said Antrim thoughtfully, "we took a long break. But do you want to know a secret? We're working on number fifty-nine right now."

Steve felt a surge of excitement. "What's it called?" he asked.

"*The Clue of the Viking's Tear*."

That sounded pretty ace.

"Jake's writing it—the old-fashioned way, on the same typewriter that was used to write *The Treasure in Trouble Harbor*." Steve looked over at the ghostwriter with the typewriter. The sleeves of his tangerine sweater were rolled up, and his arms were folded across his broad chest. His head was down, and he seemed deep in thought. Then, suddenly, he sat up straight, pulled down his sleeves, and starting pounding away furiously at the keyboard. The keys clicked and the bell clanged in a wonderful cacophony.

"That, boys, is what inspiration sounds like," said Antrim.

Soon the ghostwriter reached the bottom of the page and pulled the sheet of bright white paper from the machine.

"Want a sneak peek?" Antrim asked.

"Sure," Steve said, the thought of reading a new Bailey Brothers book almost eclipsing his disappointment about Bart.

The ghostwriter handed the paper to Antrim, who handed it to Steve. Dana looked over his shoulder and both boys read.

```
raged and the wind whipped
outside the Baileys' refuge in the
cliffs. The boys removed their
snowshoes and took stock of their
possessions.
    "Four flares, a box of matches,
and two cod sandwiches," lamented
Shawn.
    Kevin managed to will a stoic
```

smile. "We still have the treasure map."

The boys built a small fire with some kindling and wood they found near the mouth of the cave, and soon they were thawing, their spirits buoyed, as always, by sandwiches.

"I sure hope Haskol isn't sore when he finds out we wrecked his plane," Kevin reflected.

"The Ice Bear Gang must have sabotaged the fuel tank, knowing we'd be flying over here," Shawn mused. "I knew there was something sneaky about that mechanic back in Reykjavik!"

"Well, Haskol won't mind as long as we find Egil Skallagrimson's treasure!" Shawn rejoined. "Well, my stars," he murmured, studying the map in the light of the flame. "Doesn't this look familiar?"

Kevin joined his brother and

peered at the map. "Speeding cheetahs! You're right. These cliffs are the last place Skallagrimson visited! This cave must be his hiding place!"

"Guess we're lucky we crashed," Shawn chuckled ruefully.

"I knew the cliffs would be a great refuge from the storm! But who could have guessed they'd be the answer to a mystery?"

Just then there was a noise.

"Someone's here," Kevin whispered.

Many pairs of eyes gleamed.

"It's a route of wolves!" cried Shawn.

The wolves approached the fire. The leader of the pack bared his teeth as he

That was the end of the page. A cliffhanger. Classic. Steve gave the paper back to the ghostwriter, who put it face down on a stack by his typewriter. "Thanks," said Steve. "It's great so far."

"Glad you like it."

"Well, Dana, Carl," said Antrim, "that concludes your tour of the B. Syndicate. Oh, wait, hold on, I almost forgot." He ran back to the stacks of red books and pulled one from the top of a shorter pile. "Here's something for you." He opened it up to its title page, scrawled something quickly, and tossed it to Steve. Steve recognized the cover: Bailey Brothers #22: *The Treasure on the Chinese Junk*. He opened it up and read the inscription.

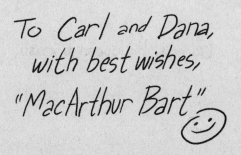

To Carl and Dana,
with best wishes,
"MacArthur Bart" ☺

Suddenly the weight of what he'd learned in the last half hour hit him again. There was no MacArthur Bart. His hero was a lie. Steve felt like the butt of a mean joke.

"Now, if you boys don't mind, we've got some work to do around here," Antrim said. He shuffled

them out the door. Steve stood in the afternoon sunlight, blinking, overwhelmed. He pulled out his notebook and a pen.

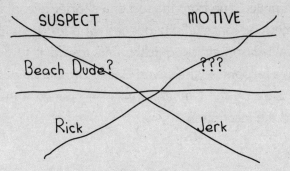

MYSTERY:
WHO KIDNAPPED MACARTHUR BART?

SUSPECT   MOTIVE

Beach Dude?   ???

Rick   Jerk

No one. He doesn't exist.

CHAPTER XXXII

A HUNCH

STEVE AND DANA sat on the curb across the street from the B. Syndicate's headquarters. Steve pulled a Jolly Rancher out of his backpack, unwrapped it, put it in his mouth, and spit it out on the pavement. No doubt about it. This was his worst day as a detective.

"So what do we do now?" Dana asked.

"We go home," Steve said.

Dana stared at Steve. "Are you kidding me?"

Steve looked at his chum. "What do you mean?"

"I mean you must be joking. We haven't solved the case."

"There is no case," Steve said. "There is no

MacArthur Bart, so he can't get kidnapped."

"So what? I want to know who those guys with guns back at the hotel were. And who was the guy with the fishing net by the mailbox? Look, I don't care whether there's a MacArthur Bart or not—I want to know who was trying to kill us. How did all this happen? We're in the middle of something."

Steve shook his head. "We're at a dead end."

Dana stood up. "Let's untangle this. This all started with a letter from MacArthur Bart. If he doesn't exist, then who wrote it?"

"I don't know." Steve thought. "Nate Rangle! It could have been Nate. He stole my letter on Monday. He opened it, read it, and decided to write back for revenge. So he called the Sea Spray and got the name of a guest, then sent me there to meet him. As a prank. But then the guest, this Snuffley, happened to be involved in something larger. Maybe he was a real criminal. Whatever—that's none of our business. I think we just stepped into a mess that has nothing to do with us. Maybe *his* gang was called the Bee Syndicate. Like the buzzing bee." Steve squinted. This wasn't right. It was like he was singing the right tune but with the wrong words.

"So Snuffley," Dana said, "he just happened to be part of a criminal organization called the Bee

Syndicate, and the group of ghostwriters that write Bailey Brothers books just happened to be called the B. Syndicate?"

"Those guys are on the up and up. Did you read those articles? Didn't you see that guy type a Bailey Brothers book?" Steve asked.

"Come on, Steve! Coincidences are the lazy detective's crutch!"

Steve stood up. He was suddenly angry. "I am not a lazy detective!"

"Then investigate this! People have been trying to kill us. It's personal now."

Steve felt his face heating up.

"Look," said Dana, "I say there's something fishy going on in that warehouse, and we need to take a closer look. Steve," said Dana solemnly, "I have a hunch."

"What?" Steve asked.

"Yep. That's right. I have a hunch."

"Seriously?"

"Seriously. There something going on with those ghostwriters. I can feel it right here." Dana pointed to his stomach.

"You've got a hunch," Steve said quietly.

Dana nodded.

Steve stood up. "Then we'd better follow it."

CHAPTER XXXIII

IT HAPPENED AT MIDNIGHT

IT WAS A MOONLESS MIDNIGHT. Steve Brixton—black-clad in sweatpants, sweatshirt, and ski cap, all purchased from a tourist kiosk in downtown San Francisco—stood shoulder to shoulder with his best chum, Dana, also in black. The only thing about their attire that was not completely stealthy and invisible was the white, reflective lettering, emblazoned across every article of clothing, reading PRISONER OF ALCATRAZ—IF FOUND, PLEASE RETURN TO THE ROCK.

They stood in the shadows, hidden from the glow of streetlamps, although no one was around to see them.

Steve held up one finger, two fingers, three, and the

boys crossed the street swiftly, in silence. Steve took out the hotel key card from his pocket and started working on the lock. Almost immediately the key card snapped in two pieces. Steve winced.

"What now?" Dana asked.

Steve motioned for Dana to follow him around the side of the building. They paused by a low window.

"In *The Tail the Tailor Told*, the Bailey Brothers are hunting down a cat burglar who breaks into apartments and jewelry stores by cutting a circle in windows and then removing the glass with suction cups. Once he's inside, he replaces the glass."

"So?"

"So that's what we'll do."

"But we don't have a burglar's kit."

"We'll improvise."

Steve scoured the ground, and it didn't take him long to find a rusty nail. "Here we go," he whispered.

There was a high, sustained squeak as Steve traced a large, lopsided circle on the pane. The nail's path left a faint white outline.

"Bingo," said Steve. "This is just what it looked like in the book."

"What about the suction cups?" Dana asked.

"The suction cups pulled the glass out toward the burglar. I'll just tap on the bottom of the circle, and then the top will come toward us, and you can catch it."

Dana frowned. Steve picked up a large rock and delicately tapped on the glass.

Nothing happened.

He tried again, with a little more force.

Still nothing.

He swung the rock, intending to give the glass a good knock.

The whole window shattered.

"We're in!" Steve said.

Steve found an old bucket and turned it upside down by the wall. The two boys used it as a step stool and gingerly climbed through window.

Steve and Dana took a few cautious steps. Shards of glass crunched beneath their feet. A pipe was leaking somewhere deep in the building. The place was deserted.

Steve flipped his flashlight on and slowly moved the beam across the room. In the pale yellow light, things that had seemed real this afternoon took on a ghostly aspect.

"Okay," said Steve. "Let's split up. I'll check out the ghostwriters' desks. Next, you look at Antrim's office. We're looking for anything that proves these guys are up to something, that they aren't who they say they are. See if you can get in that locked filing cabinet."

"How am I supposed to see in the dark?" Dana asked.

Steve smiled. He reached into his backpack and pulled out a flashlight. "I bought this for you at Walgreens today when you were in the candy aisle. It's a present. Every sleuth needs one."

Dana took the flashlight and turned it on. "Thanks," he said. "But I'm not a sleuth."

Dana disappeared silently into the maze of Bailey Brothers books. Steve turned and crept over to the desks. He paused. He needed to search methodically. He'd start at the desk closest to him and work back, checking all the drawers. Then he'd look at the ghostwriters' computers.

But first he would take a peek at that new Bailey Brothers book. Just to see what was going to happen with the wolves.

He went over to the stack of papers next to the typewriter and turned it face up. The page he'd read this morning was right on top. Steve reread the last bit to get in the mood:

"Someone's here," Kevin
whispered.
Many pairs of eyes gleamed.
"It's a route of wolves!" cried
Shawn.

The wolves approached the fire. The leader of the pack bared his teeth as he

Steve flipped to the next page:

raged and the wind whipped outside the Baileys' refuge in the cliffs. The boys removed their snowshoes and took stock of their possessions.

"Four flares, a box of matches, and two cod sandwiches," lamented Shawn.

Kevin managed to will a stoic smile. "We still have the treasure map."

The boys built a small fire with some kindling and wood they found near the mouth of the cave, and soon they were thawing, their spirits buoyed, as always, by sandwiches.

Steve stopped. This was how the last page had started. He scanned down to the bottom. This page was identical to the one he'd just read. He flipped to the next page. The same. Steve rifled through the thick stack of paper. Every page was the same. This wasn't a new Bailey Brothers book. It was the same piece of a story typed over and over again.

The ghostwriter was a fake! The B. Syndicate was a front!

But a front for what? And if the B. Syndicate hadn't written the Bailey Brothers books, who had?

Steve's heartbeat sped. He had to show Dana. He tucked the manuscript under his arm and ran back through the warehouse and up to Antrim's office. Dana was crouched behind Antrim's desk, peering into an open drawer. "Nothing so far," he said. "I'm trying to find a key to that cabinet."

"Dana, check it out." Steve shoved his find in front of his chum's face. "Notice anything weird?"

Dana read through the first page. When he got to the next one, his eyes widened.

"They're all the same," Steve said. "You were right! There's something weird going on here."

"This is—"

Dana was interrupted by a sound from down in the warehouse: the whine of the front door opening. Someone was coming inside.

CHAPTER XXXIV

EAVESDROPPING

STEVE AND DANA CLICKED off their lights and dove for cover against the half wall of Antrim's office.

"What do we do?" Dana whispered.

"Just wait. Maybe they don't know we're in here."

"I hope they don't see the broken window."

Two voices became clear, ringing through the empty warehouse. Steve recognized them: the doorman and Henry.

"Just seems like a waste," Henry said.

"Yeah, but you know the boss. Cautious to the point of paranoid. Apparently the kid went to the cops today."

"So what? The cops have been by before. That's why we have this place."

"Yeah, but he says as long as this Brixton kid's snooping around, the whole operation's at risk."

So Antrim was scared. Steve felt a rush of satisfaction.

"Plus," said the doorman, "he's mad at us for not getting the job done in Ocean Park."

"Well, why didn't they just grab the kids when they were in here today?"

"They thought they were just fans. Apparently, Brixton used a fake name. Carter or something. They still don't know how the kids found out about the B. Syndicate."

"And they're not gonna."

Steve wanted to laugh.

"Well, come on, let's get this done."

The two boys sat, their backs pressed hard against the wall, listening intently and clenching their teeth. Sometimes they heard footsteps, sometimes they heard rustling, and sometimes they heard nothing at all.

Finally the doorman spoke. "All right," he said quickly. "Let's get out of here."

The front door clanged shut.

"Are they gone?" said Dana.

"Maybe," said Steve. "Or maybe it's a trap. Let's wait five minutes."

Sure enough, soon there was the sound of more rustling, and then cracking, like chairs being broken over someone's knee.

"What's happening?" Dana hissed.

Steve didn't know, and he hated that he didn't know. His brain was divided into two halves: the half that wanted to peek over the wall and see what was going on and the half that wanted to stay hidden forever.

He stared straight ahead, thinking. Then he noticed something unusual.

The window behind Antrim's desk, across from him, was flickering, like it was reflecting the lights of a thousand flashlights.

He nudged Dana with his elbow. "Look."

"How many people are down there?" Dana asked.

Steve was sweating. Normally he didn't sweat much. He wiped his face with his sweatshirt.

All right. That was it. Steve had to look. He had to know. If there was an army of ghostwriters down in the warehouse, then it was better to find that out now and think of a plan.

He turned around and slowly rose up to take a peek. As soon as his face was above the half wall, a blast of heat burned his eyes. It was like he had opened an oven door.

There was no army of ghostwriters.

But the warehouse was on fire.

A thousand Bailey Brothers books went up in flames.

CHAPTER XXXV

FIRESTORM

"FIRE!" SHOUTED STEVE.

Dana popped up next to him.

"Fire!" shouted Dana.

They squinted and watched as the fire spread across the warehouse floor. Steve had had no idea fire moved so quickly. Orange flames engulfed whole swaths of the space below. Towers of red Bailey Brothers novels burned, sending grayish-brown clouds of ash and heat billowing to the ceiling. It was mesmerizing. Dana and Steve watched, transfixed and horrified. Hot smoke poured upward. It was like a liquid, thick and quick-moving, constantly in motion.

The smoke hit their faces, hot and dry and foul. It was like being downwind of the world's biggest campfire. They ducked back down.

"What do we do?" Dana shouted. The fire was loud. Who knew fires were so loud? "The fire's between us and the door!"

"I don't know!"

"What does the handbook say?"

Steve pulled out the handbook and looked up "fire" in the index, then went to page 122. "'Stop, drop, and roll!'" Steve read out loud.

"That's what you do if you're *on* fire!" Dana screamed.

"Well, that's all it says!" Steve stashed the handbook back in his backpack.

The whole room was heating up fast, and smoke rushed in. Steve took off his sweatshirt and put it over his face. He had never been this hot in his life. His skin stung, ten times worse than the sunburn he'd gotten at the beach last August. The wall the boys were leaning against was radiating heat. Keeping low and staying close to each other, Steve and Dana crawled to the middle of the office. It was getting hard to see. The beam of Steve's flashlight only traveled a few feet before getting lost in a cloud of smoke.

Down on the floor there was a sound like gunshots popping off.

Through the haze Steve saw that things in Antrim's office had begun to catch fire. Over to his right, blue arcs of electricity jumped and danced. The air was hot and thick and tasted like plastic. Steve couldn't see a thing. His flashlight was now useless. He reached out in the dark with his left hand and felt Dana's arm. He grabbed it tight.

"We're trapped!" Dana said.

Steve was disoriented. Lost. He didn't know which way they had come from. He just lay there, breathing into his shirt. He couldn't give up. He could not give up. But what could he do?

Sirens. Sirens getting closer. For the first time all week Steve was glad to hear sirens.

Would the firemen be able to find them? Would they even be looking for kids in an old warehouse?

There was a glimmer of light off to Steve's left. It got stronger. Lots of lights, flashing, like strobes.

"The window!" Steve shouted as loud as he could, but now he couldn't even hear himself. The fire was just too loud. Things were falling and cracking and breaking and roaring.

He pulled on Dana's arm and put Dana's hand on his back. Dana grabbed Steve's shirt. Steve got up on his hands and knees and started crawling toward the flashing lights. Dana followed. They got to Antrim's desk and crawled around it to the window. The world outside seemed like a blur of bright lights, red trucks, and snarled hoses. Steve stood up. It was a lot hotter on his feet. He groped around in the dark for something heavy.

There. He felt it. Something wooden. Antrim's chair. Steve picked it up and hurled it mightily at the window. There was the sound of shattering glass and a blast of cool air. The smoke poured outward. Steve saw Dana a few feet to his right. He reached out.

The decision to jump out a window had never been easier.

Blindly, hand in hand, they leapt.

They fell down hard on a fireman who was trying to knock down the back door.

Steve, Dana, and the fireman all tumbled to the ground.

CHAPTER XXXVI

TROUBLE IN THE HOSPITAL

"YOU BOYS ARE IN A LOT OF TROUBLE," said Detective Taylor.

She was sitting in a chair in Steve and Dana's hospital room. It was morning, and the room was bright and sunny. A mural stretched around the walls showing a train being driven by Mickey Mouse, except you could tell the mural was not officially sanctioned by Disney, because certain features on Mickey's face were slightly off: His coloring was too orange, and his snout was a little long. Plus Bugs Bunny (who for some reason was yellow) was riding in the caboose. Mickey and Bugs only got together in these weird hand-done paintings you found in pediatric wards and dentists' offices. Impostor cartoon murals always made Steve vaguely uneasy.

Steve and Dana sat straight up in bed. Until Detective Taylor walked in, they had been watching TV. They felt fine, although they both smelled like smoke. Last night they'd been taken to the hospital for monitoring, and the nurse had told them this morning they were ready to go.

"Do you two want to tell me what you were doing at that warehouse last night?" Detective Taylor asked.

"That was the B. Syndicate headquarters!"

"I know that now," said Detective Taylor. "And the B. Syndicate is a book-writing collective. Not a criminal gang."

"So they say," said Steve.

"And I don't know why I did this, but I looked up MacArthur Bart. No one with that name is currently living in the United States. It's a pen name. And apparently a lot of people already know this. A couple of guys around the station were big Bailey Brothers fans, and they all remembered where they were when they first found out that MacArthur Bart didn't exist."

"Don't you think it's a pretty big coincidence—"

"I think it's a pretty big coincidence that a building

you guys broke into last night caught on fire."

"Exactly!" said Steve.

Detective Taylor just looked at them.

"Wait," said Steve. "You don't think . . ."

"That we . . . ," said Dana.

"Arson?" said Detective Taylor. "It was the first thing that crossed my mind. But it looks like it was caused by an electrical short. I guess the lesson there is that sometimes a coincidence is really just a coincidence."

Steve was about to tell her about the conversation they'd overheard before the fire started, but he thought better of it. No need to complicate things. Detective Taylor would never believe them. They just needed to get out of there and finish the case. The manuscript for the new Bailey Brothers book would have been destroyed in the fire. The Syndicate's headquarters was in ashes. There was a lot of sleuthing to be done.

The police detective looked at the boys for a few seconds and then said, "Of course, you two were trespassing."

Dana groaned.

"But I talked to a Mr. Antrim, and he doesn't want to press charges."

Steve was relieved, but suspicious.

"And I called your parents—"

"How'd you find their number?" Steve asked.

"I called the number on your business card." Detective Taylor said.

"See, I need my own phone line," Steve said to Dana.

Dana nodded.

"Your parents are very upset," Detective Taylor continued, "Apparently you two were supposed to be in San Diego, at a debate tournament?"

Steve and Dana didn't say anything.

"Steve, your dad is here to see you."

Steve was confused. "My dad?"

A grinning man in a tan uniform stepped into the doorway.

Great. It was Rick.

"Well, if it isn't the debate champions."

"Rick's not my dad," said Steve.

"You boys are in a lot of trouble," said Rick.

"We heard."

"Your parents are none too pleased. None too pleased at all. They sent me to take you home."

"Why did they send you, Rick?" asked Steve.

"Well, I offered. See, there are a couple things I'd like to talk to you boys about, and I thought a long drive might be a good opportunity to get some answers. So once we heard that you were okay, your parents decided to entrust you to a responsible officer of the law."

Rick smiled.

"Me," he said.

Detective Taylor seemed less than impressed.

"I can't believe you thought he was my dad," said Steve.

"Let's go, boys," said Rick. "We need to talk."

CHAPTER XXXVII

GOING HOME

THE THREE OF THEM SAT shoulder to shoulder in the front of Rick's truck, driving through the streets of San Francisco. Dana, a true chum, sat in the middle. Both boys were morose about their investigation's abrupt ending.

"You guys smell like a campfire," Rick said.

"Yeah, the nurse said that will last for about a week," Dana replied.

"Oh," said Rick, rolling down a window.

"So, while you guys were supposed to be in San Diego," Rick said after a long silence, "some weird stuff happened at the Sea Spray Waterfront Hotel."

Dana got tense.

"Oh, yeah," said Steve. "I heard that place is pretty nice. What's been going on?"

"You heard it's pretty ni—hey, that's good, Steve. Well, let's see. There was a huge shoot-out by the pool."

"Crazy," said Steve.

"Really wild," said Dana.

"You know, Rick," said Steve, "feel free to tell me about this stuff if you want my professional advice, but I really can't solve all your cases for you."

"I'm not . . . You're just . . . Look, the hotel manager reports two kids acting suspicious at the front desk right before the shoot-out happened. One blond, one with brown hair."

"Hmm," said Steve. "Maybe they're kids in our school?"

"Nate Rangle has brown hair," Dana said.

Rick's grip on the steering wheel tightened. "And the day before, a kid was hanging around the hotel."

"So?"

"A kid detective."

"Could be any kid detective."

"The clerk thinks his name was Steve."

"Oh," said Steve.

"But you've never been to the Sea Spray Waterfront

Hotel," said Rick, "so it's probably some other amateur sleuth named Steve."

"I'm not really an amateur, Rick. And, yes, maybe I have been by the hotel."

"Why?" said Rick sharply, taking his eyes off the road to look at Steve for a second.

"Confidential," said Steve.

"Why don't you just tell me what's going on, Steve? I can help you."

"Like on my last case?" Steve said. "When you arrested me?"

"I didn't arrest you."

"You would have, if I hadn't stolen your police car." Dana snorted.

"Look, Steve," said Rick. "I'm sorry I tried to arrest you. I made a mistake. But we need to trust each other now. I can help you."

Steve was silent. Rick pulled over to the curb in front of Ghirardelli Square.

"The curb's red, Rick," said Steve.

"It's all right. I'm a cop."

Steve rolled his eyes.

"You guys stay in the car," Rick said. "I'm going to run in and grab some chocolate for your mom. She loves this stuff. It'll put her in a better mood."

Rick hopped out of the truck, paused, and turned

back to Steve. "Does she like milk chocolate or dark?"

"Isn't that your job, Rick?"

She liked milk chocolate.

Rick shook his head. "Hey, I'm trying to help you out here, man."

Just as Rick was closing the door, Dana said, "Hey, Rick, will you leave us your keys so we can listen to the radio?"

Rick hesitated for a moment.

"Rick," said Steve, "I'm sorry I stole your police car. I was wrong. We need to trust each other."

Rick squinted at Steve, then nodded slowly.

"Please let us listen to the radio so we're not bored out of our minds."

Rick smiled. "All right, Steve. Yeah. We can trust each other."

"When Mom hears that, she'll really be in a good mood."

Rick laughed. He tossed Dana the keys.

"Now, when I come back," said Rick, "let's the three of us have a talk, as friends." He shut the door. Dana put Rick's keys in the ignition and turned them to power the radio.

"You're listening to 103.1, the Wave, smooth jazz on the California coast," said a velvety voice. Then some guy started playing clarinet, accompanied by a tinny keyboard.

"This music sucks," said Dana.

"Seriously," said Steve. The thing was, smooth jazz wasn't jazz. It wasn't really even that smooth.

Dana flipped through stations while Steve played with the button that controlled the windows. Something caught his attention in the rearview mirror. He turned around to make sure his eyes weren't playing tricks on him.

"Dana," said Steve. "It's the doorman!"

Dana whipped around and looked out of the truck's back window. Sure enough, the doorman was walking out of a mini-mart, carrying a bag of groceries. He was wearing tan slacks and a turquoise sweater.

"He's dressed like a ghostwriter!"

The ghostwriter loaded the bag into the trunk of his car.

"Where's he going with those groceries?" Dana asked.

"Let's find out," said Steve.

Steve climbed over Dana and took a seat behind the wheel.

He turned the key in the ignition.

Rick's truck started up.

CHAPTER XXXVIII

BIG CITY CHASE

"OKAY," SAID STEVE. "You get on the floor and press the gas and brake pedals when I tell you."

"Wait, why?"

"Because I can't work the pedals and see the road at the same time."

"Yeah, but why do I have to be the one on the floor?"

"Because I already know how to drive."

Dana sighed and slipped down to the floor. Steve kneeled on the driver's seat, found the gearshift, and put the truck in reverse.

"Gas!" said Steve.

The car jumped backward.

"Brake!" said Steve. "Gently!"

He couldn't really make out Dana's reply.

The ghostwriter drove past them in the opposite direction.

Steve turned the wheel hard to the left and shifted into drive. "Gas!" he shouted.

The truck leapt into the street and made a hard U-turn. Oncoming traffic slammed to a halt. Horns blared.

"Brake!"

"Gas!"

"Gas!"

Steve worked the wheel and got the car moving in the right lane.

"How's it going down there?"

"It's gross. There are lots of jelly beans, and they're covered in lint."

"Well, you're doing an ace job."

"Thanks."

"Brake!"

The truck screeched to a halt.

"You've got to be gentler," said Steve.

"Don't be a backseat driver," said Dana.

"I'm not. I'm a driver's-seat driver."

The ghostwriter's car was way ahead of them,

stopped at the intersection. If the light hadn't turned red, they would have lost him.

The light turned green.

"We're going to have to do some aggressive driving," Steve said.

"Great," mumbled Dana.

Steve's mom always said driving in San Francisco was tricky. She was right, although Steve didn't have much to compare it to. He drove right up behind the cars ahead of him, swerving in and out of lanes, trying to gain on the gray sedan.

Steve followed the ghostwriter onto Marina Avenue. They headed toward a highway on-ramp.

"Hit the gas hard," said Steve. "We're getting on the freeway."

Steve watched the speedometer climb: 30, 40, 50, 60. "There," he said. Steve had never driven on a freeway before. He liked it. Steve was concentrating so hard on the gray car, and also on trying not to crash, that it took him a few seconds to realize where he was. "We're driving across the Golden Gate Bridge!" said Steve. To his right the bay teemed with brightly colored sails. To his left there was only a wild expanse of ocean. "It's amazing!"

"Great," said Dana on the floor.

The gray car took the first exit after the bridge.

Steve piloted the truck across the Golden Gate.

Steve followed. "Slowly, Dana," he said. "Let's follow at a distance."

They were on a two-lane road that wound through a national park. Steve let the ghostwriter get far ahead—he didn't want the guy to figure out he was being followed. A stretch of blue opened up before them; they were headed toward the ocean. The road curved gently right when it reached the sea and wound along the coast. The gray car turned round a blind curve.

"Ease off the gas," Steve said. "This turn's pretty sharp."

Steve worked the wheel and guided the truck around the curve.

"Stop!" he shouted.

Dana slammed on the brakes. The truck skidded and stopped.

The ghostwriter's car had disappeared.

CHAPTER XXXIX

THE VANISHING SEDAN

STEVE AND DANA PARKED the truck by the side of the road and got out.

"Where'd he go?" said Dana.

"Secret road," said Steve.

"What?"

"Secret road." Steve pulled out *The Bailey Brothers' Detective Handbook*, which has a chapter on high-speed chases:

> Shawn and Kevin are super drivers, but crooks can be tricky behind the wheel. Smugglers and car thieves often

build secret roads off the main highway, invisible to law-abiding citizens. When these speedy creeps are chased by police, they turn down the secret roads and disappear! But Shawn and Kevin know what to look for, and so should you: The entrances to secret roads are usually after sharp curves, and they're covered up by fake shrubs, or blocked off by a conspiratorial farmer's tractor! Keep your eyes, peeled, sleuths! Don't be a chump.

There were no farms nearby. There was a forest, but that was a ways back from the highway.

"There must be a secret road here somewhere," Steve said, looking down the cliff at the ocean below. White froth bloomed on the water's surface and disappeared in translucent puffs.

"This is ridiculous," Dana said, coming up next to his friend. "There is no such thing as a secret road. We lost him, okay?"

The roar of the ocean obscured the sound of the man coming up behind them, so Steve didn't realize what was happening until it was too late. Steve saw a hand, holding a cloth, in his periphery. Of course. It wasn't a coincidence that they'd run into a ghostwriter.

It was a trap. Steve knew what was about to happen.

Time slowed down. In the moments before the cloth was placed over Steve's mouth and nose, Steve noticed many tiny details.

The cloth was red.

The man's sweater sleeve, rolled up, was turquoise.

On his forearm there was a tattoo. Steve just had time to read "rage will always be my last refuge" before he blacked out.

CHAPTER XL

CAPTURED! AGAIN!

WHEN STEVE CAME TO, his hands and feet were trussed up with rough ropes. It was dark—the only light came from a sputtering candle on a rocky ledge above him. He was cold, and so was the ground he was sitting on. His back was against a wet wall, and the air was thick and damp. The soft plinking sound of dripping water came from all sides. There was no doubt about it. Steve was in a sea cave. And his backpack was gone.

Dana was heaped on the ground to Steve's right. Steve nudged him a couple of times with his feet, and he saw his friend groggily open his eyes.

"Where are we?" Dana asked.

"Who are you?"

Before Steve could answer, someone behind him spoke. "Trapped. In a criminal lair."

Steve adjusted his position so he could turn toward the voice. A large man with a white beard and salt-and-pepper hair was sitting a few feet away. He was wearing a thick sweater with a large turtleneck and a black eye patch over his right eye. His arms were behind his back, and his legs were bound. The man was smiling, and his smile was warm and wise.

"Who are you?" Dana asked.

Steve knew what the man would say before he said it.

"I'm MacArthur Bart."

CHAPTER XLI

WELCOME NEWS

"You do exist!" Steve said.

"Of course I do," said MacArthur Bart. "I wrote you that letter."

Steve's heart was happy. He wanted to shake his hero's hand, and would have, except for the ropes.

"I'm glad to see you, Steve. Although I wish we were meeting under better circumstances. And you must be Steve's friend Dana."

"Hey," said Dana. "Good to meet you."

MacArthur Bart sniffed. "What smells like a campfire?"

"We do," Dana said. "What's going on? Where are we?"

MacArthur Bart smiled sadly. "We've all been kidnapped by the B. Syndicate."

"The B. Syndicate's a front!" said Steve. "They claim they wrote the Bailey Brothers books!"

MacArthur Bart's smile disappeared. "I know. Those ghostwriters are nothing more than mercenaries. Smugglers, thieves, and thugs. That's why I got in touch with you—I was hoping you could help me deal with them."

"What do you mean?" Steve asked.

Bart chuckled. "I suppose I have a little explaining to do."

"I'll say," Dana said.

"Well, let's start at the beginning." Bart leaned back against the limestone wall. "When I was a young man, not so much older than the two of you, I had to support myself. And so I wrote my first book. It was a mystery for children, about two teen sleuths who recover a sunken treasure in the bayside town where they live. The first Bailey Brothers mystery. It was very popular, and I wrote more. Many more. Three books a year for the next ten years.

"Now, boys, like many writers I am shy, even

private by nature. I had a small house in the forests north of San Francisco, where I did my writing in isolation. With success came fame, but I wanted no part of fame. And so whenever I went out in public, I did so under an assumed name."

"A. C. Snuffley," said Steve.

"Exactly!" said Bart. "I've used many fake names, but that has always been one of my favorites. And so, even as a nation of children grew to love MacArthur Bart, nobody knew that I was he. And then, after fifty-eight books, fifty-eight thrilling and action-packed Bailey Brothers mysteries, I ran out of ideas. I cobbled together *The Bailey Brothers' Detective Handbook* by pulling tricks and tips from the previous books. But the handbook was the last book I ever wrote.

"I had writer's block. I could come up with bits and pieces of Bailey Brothers stories, sure, but I couldn't finish anything. A year passed. Then five years passed. And soon I gave up. I became more and more reclusive. I threw out my television set, stopped reading the newspaper. That was a long time ago."

"What about the ghostwriters?" Steve asked.

"I was getting to that. A few years after I stopped writing, I received a visitor: a young man who called himself Jack Antrim. I don't know how he found me, but I was sorry he did. He was a gangster, plain and simple, the leader of a crime ring. And he had a bold plan. Every illegal enterprise needs a legitimate front. A fake business helps you launder money and throws off the police. Well, this Antrim wanted to hide his gang behind a literary syndicate. It was brilliant. Who's going to look closely at a bunch of writers for hire? I can't imagine a less interesting group of people than writers."

Steve saw where this was going and chimed in. "So he created the story that his gang wrote the Bailey Brothers Mysteries!"

"Exactly. A completely legitimate front."

"But why'd you go along with it?" Steve asked.

"I was scared. He said he'd kill me if I went public. Besides, I had money, and, like I said, I didn't want attention."

"But that's cowardly!" Dana said. Bart winced.

It hurt Steve to hear his hero called a coward, but he couldn't disagree.

"You're right, Dana. It was cowardly. But a few months ago I was stocking up on supplies in the town near my home and I saw a magazine cover promising an article on 'the Real MacArthur Bart.' I picked it up, of course, and there was a picture of Jack Antrim smiling back at me. It was a bunch of hogwash about his grandfather and the B. Syndicate, and it all made me so furious I started shaking. I decided enough was enough. And when I received your letter about solving that mystery in Ocean Park—the publisher still forwards my mail to a P.O. box I keep under the name Philip Snatterly—I knew you could help me. So I came to visit you. But the B. Syndicate got to me before we could meet."

"And so now here we are," said Steve. "Sorry we couldn't be more help."

"Oh, I don't know about that," said Bart. "I could always use the help of a couple detectives."

"Actually, Steve's the only detective. I'm just Dana."

"How can we help you?" Steve asked.

"You can help me escape," said Bart, his eye twinkling.

"But we're all tied up," said Steve.

"Come on, Steve," said Bart. *"The Bailey Brothers' Detective Handbook*. Chapter sixteen: 'Escaping from Your Bonds.'"

"'Find a keen blade or a piece of slate and secretly saw the ropes against the sharp edge,'" said Steve.

"You forgot 'jagged limestone formations,'" Bart said. He paused, straining, then smiled. "There."

He brought his arms in front of his chest and rubbed his wrists.

Bart was free!

CHAPTER XLII

A DARING PLAN

MACARTHUR BART UNTIED Dana and Steve quickly. The boys stood up. Steve's muscles were sore, and his head ached.

"Listen up," said Bart. "We're in a small room off the cave's main chamber. That's where the ghostwriters have their hideout. There's a narrow passageway that connects this cavern to theirs. Are you boys following me?"

Steve and Dana nodded.

"Now," Bart continued, "there are usually only two ghostwriters here at a time. Our best plan is to lure them in here and then ambush them. I'll take one; you two take the other."

"How are we going to do that?" Dana asked. "It's not exactly a fair fight."

Dana had a point. Bart seemed pretty strong, especially for an old man, but Steve and Dana didn't exactly have the best record when it came to throwdowns.

"I used to box," said Bart, "and I still train regularly." Steve was beyond impressed. "I'll try to look out for you two. But if you can, hit these guys in the solar plexus."

It was time to settle this once and for all.

"Mr. Bart," said Steve, "where is the solar plexus?"

Bart smiled and pointed to his abdomen.

"Why didn't you just say stomach?" Dana asked.

"Because," said Bart, "the simplest way to say things is seldom the most enjoyable."

"Yeah, come on, Dana," said Steve. "Solar plexus sounds completely ace."

The trio moved over to the mouth of the passageway. Bart positioned himself on one side; Dana and Steve crouched on the other.

"Ready?" asked MacArthur Bart.

"Yeah," said Steve.

"I don't know," said Dana.

"Help!" shouted Bart. "Help! One of the boys is injured! He's bleeding!"

Steve heard footsteps and saw the walls of the passageway glow orange with the light of a flashlight. Someone was approaching.

CHAPTER XLIII

AMBUSH

JACK ANTRIM STEPPED out of the passageway.

"What—" was all he managed to say before MacArthur Bart landed an uppercut to his chin. Antrim dropped his flashlight, reeled back, and put his fists up. "Scott! Get in here! They're trying to escape!"

Bart and Antrim moved into the center of the cave, punching and counterpunching, dodging and circling.

Another set of footfalls echoed.

"Let's come at him from both sides," Dana said hurriedly. He repositioned himself on the other side of the passageway.

In the dim light of Antrim's flashlight, Steve saw the

second ghostwriter emerge into the room. Even in the dark, Steve recognized him: It was the doorman.

Dana screamed. The doorman turned toward Steve's chum. Steve panicked. Now that the brute's back was to Steve, how could he punch his solar plexus? Dana launched himself at the ghostwriter, and the man came stumbling back toward Steve, who was still crouching. First the doorman, then Dana, tripped over Steve and came crashing onto the cavern floor. There was a dull thump.

Steve reached for Antrim's flashlight and shone it on the pair of bodies. Dana turned back to the light, his eyes huge. The doorman wasn't moving. "He hit his head on a stalagmite," Dana said.

"I think you mean a stalactite," said Steve.

"No," said Dana. "I mean a stalagmite."

Steve thought about it for a second. Dana was right. Too bad. "Whatever," Steve said.

"I think we sort of kayoed him," Steve said.

"I think we totally kayoed him," said Dana.

Steve stared at the man on the ground. Even though the doorman had been ready to fight them seconds earlier, and shooting at them a couple of days ago, Steve felt a little worried about him.

"Is he breathing?" Steve asked.

"I don't know," said Dana.

Steve crouched down next to the man on the ground.

"What are you doing?" Dana asked.

"Checking his pulse," Steve said. He saw the

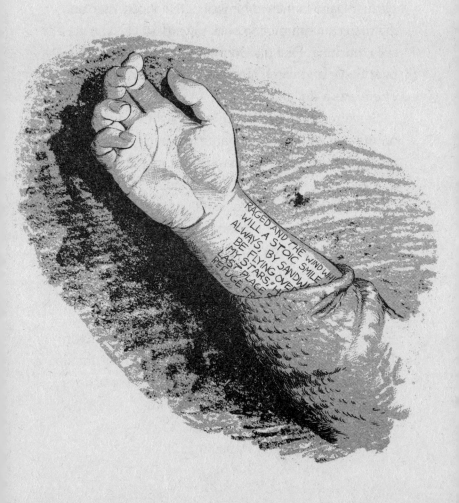

tattoo, "rage will always be my last refuge." But Steve froze when he rolled up the man's sleeve. The tattoo continued.

"He's fine," said Dana. "I can see him breathing."

But Steve still stared at the man's arm. He remembered the ghostwriter from yesterday, staring down at his crossed arms. So this was how these thugs masqueraded as writers—their tattoos were permanent cheat sheets that helped them write a page from the Bailey Brothers on command.

Behind him, Steve heard a man groan and drop to the floor.

CHAPTER XLIV

AN UNDERGROUND ESCAPE

STEVE TURNED AND POINTED the flashlight toward the sound. Antrim was on the ground, moaning softly. Bart, the sleeves of his sweater rolled up and his hands balled in fists, was still standing.

"Come on, boys," said Bart. "Let's get out of here."

The two boys followed the writer down the passage-way and into the main chamber of the cave. A series of electric lamps lined the walls. Steve was dumbstruck. Four shiny sports cars were parked in the middle of the cavern. Ornately framed paintings, wrapped in plastic, leaned against a rock column. Marble statues stood next to stalagmites. Wooden crates were everywhere. It looked like an underground bank vault.

"What's with all the treasure?" Dana asked.

"This must be where the B. Syndicate hides all their loot," Steve replied. Something on a small card table in the middle of the chamber caught Steve's eye. There, next to a pile of magazines, was Steve's green backpack. He ran for it.

"Steve!" shouted Bart. "What are you doing? We need to get out of here."

"My backpack!" Steve said.

"We don't have time," said Bart.

"Just leave it," Dana said.

But Steve kept running. He got to the table, slipped on a wet rock, picked himself up, and put on his backpack. Then he ran back to Bart and Dana.

"That was so dumb," Dana said.

"I need my detective kit," Steve replied.

"Never mind that," said Bart. "I overheard the ghostwriters say there were two ways out of this cave." He pointed to the right. A faint breeze came from that direction. "That way leads to the ocean. The other way leads to an opening up on the cliffs."

"Let's go up," Steve said.

Bart nodded. They worked their way toward the back of the chamber, which narrowed to a steeply sloping pathway. Soon the electric lamps ended. Steve got out his flashlight and handed Antrim's to Bart.

Bart led the way, Dana was second, and Steve brought up the rear. He hoped he could run like that when he was Bart's age. He wished he could run like that now. Steve couldn't believe he was escaping from a crime syndicate after sort of rescuing his hero. As he jogged in the near dark, he played the past few days' events over in his mind. Like the Bailey Brothers would say, this had been a dilly of a case. Steve had never known what that meant, but he thought he did now.

After following the passageway up for what seemed like miles, Steve felt cool air on his face.

"We're getting near the opening," Bart said.

And he was right. Soon Steve could make out the silhouettes of trees and the starry sky ahead.

And then they were outside again. They kept going for a few minutes and then paused for a rest. Steve, Dana, and MacArthur Bart paused by the trunk of a tall tree and caught their breath.

"We did it," Bart said.

Dana was grinning.

Bart stroked his beard. "We'll rest here for a couple more minutes, then find our way to the road, which should be over that way. We'll try to find a ranger and get a ride back to San Francisco. Then we'll figure out how to take out this gang once and for all."

That plan sounded great.

Steve reached into his backpack and pulled out a pen and the copy of *The Treasure on the Chinese Junk* Antrim had given him. "Mr. Bart," Steve said, "now that we're out of there, would you do me a favor? Would you sign this book for me?"

"Steve," said Dana, his smile gone, "I don't think now is the best time for this. We're still kind of escaping right now."

"Those guys are all kayoed," Steve said. "I can't stand thinking that this book is signed by a ghostwriter."

MacArthur Bart laughed. "Sure, Steve." Bart winked at Dana. "Don't worry, I sign fast." He scribbled something and gave it back.

Steve studied the book in the moonlight.

To Carl and Dana,
with best wishes,
"MacArthur Bart"

FOR STEVE BRIXTON
A TRUE SLEUTH, A REAL HERO,
AN ACE CHUM
MacArthur Bart

Steve smiled.

Dana shook his head. "First the backpack, now this. It's like you want to get caught."

Steve wheeled toward his friend. "For your information, going back for the backpack was important. The Nichols Diamond is in my backpack, okay?"

Dana's eyes grew large.

"What," Steve said. "You think I'd be stupid enough to hide it in my room?"

Dana shook his head. He was looking past Steve.

Steve turned around.

MacArthur Bart was holding a gun.

CHAPTER XLV

FIENDISHLY BETRAYED

"OH, NO," SAID STEVE. "No no no no no."

"I'm afraid so, Steve," said MacArthur Bart.

"So you're not MacArthur Bart!" said Dana.

Steve shook his head slowly. "No. He is."

"Yes, I am," said Bart. "You're figuring it out, aren't you, detective?"

"I'm not," said Dana.

"This was all you," said Steve.

"What?" asked Dana. "What's going on?"

Steve ignored him. "You made up this whole kidnapping business." Bart nodded. Steve continued,

Steve couldn't take his eyes off the gun in his face.

"We didn't just escape. That was all just a dance back there, a trick to get the diamond. You're the thief who broke into Fairview's mansion."

"Very good," said Bart.

Steve put his hands over his eyes. "And I tipped you off to the plant in the drill."

"You did?" Dana asked.

"He did," Bart said. "In his weekly letter to me. I was dismayed to read that you'd cracked my scheme for smuggling the diamond out past Fairview's security system. Impressed, but dismayed. But I'm so glad you clued me in about the plant. You were so proud of yourself, Steve!"

Steve slouched.

"You lied to us!" said Dana. "You're not a writer! You're a crook."

Bart turned. "I'm both," he said. "The story I told you in the cave was true. Up to a point. I am a very private person. And I did write the Bailey Brothers books—all of them. And I did get writer's block. But that's where the truth ends.

"You see, I'd become accustomed to a certain lifestyle—nice food, exotic travel, et cetera, et cetera. You boys probably wouldn't understand."

Steve hated it when people said that.

"And though the Bailey Brothers books were

successful, wildly successful, I'd need to keep writing them if I wanted to keep the lifestyle up. But like I said, I had bits and pieces of a story but couldn't finish a book.

"And that's when I had an idea. As a mystery writer I was rather uniquely skilled at devising clever crimes. Why not start committing some? Crimes for which I could never be caught.

"After years of creative despair I was inspired. My first idea was my most brilliant: I destroyed all records of my existence. That was a lot easier to do back then; a simple fire in a courthouse basement and you could make all traces of your identity vanish. Then I leaked the story about MacArthur Bart's never existing to the newspapers. The name was simply a pseudonym, the story went, used by ghostwriters who wrote the Bailey Brothers mysteries for a hundred dollars a book. I hired a bunch of cons to pose as ghostwriters—they also became the muscle in my organization.

"Of course, my publisher tried—and still tries—to keep the fact that I don't exist quiet. Kids like to think there's a real MacArthur Bart. But anyone who does a little digging finds out that I don't exist. And how can the police catch a man who doesn't exist?"

"So you're the one who tattooed the Bailey Brothers stories on the ghostwriters' arms," Steve said.

"Yes," said Bart. "I thought it would be important that my writers actually be able to write, just in case cops or reporters came snooping around. So I had them memorize a page of an abandoned Bailey Brothers story. But it turns out hardened criminals aren't necessarily great memorizers, and they ended up cheating and writing the lines down on their arms every day. That seemed inefficient. So: the tattoos."

"Wait. What about all the other books? Have you been ghostwriting celebrity autobiographies in your spare time?"

Bart laughed. "No. The thugs write those. Have you ever read a pop star's memoir? They all read like they were written by goons."

"You're crazy," Dana said.

"No," said Bart. "Just cautious. And that's why I've never been caught. I successfully perpetrated grand robberies and wild swindles. My ghostwriters and I have done everything. Smuggling, counterfeiting, stealing paintings and jewels. I have a weakness for rare and valuable treasures. And then I received your letter a while back, the one with the newspaper clipping about your little detective agency."

Steve felt furious. The Brixton Brothers Detective Agency was not little.

Bart laughed. "Yes, that was the first valuable letter

you sent me. On the back of that clipping was a little squib about Fairview and his marvelous diamond. And I knew it had to be mine."

Dana interrupted. "What's a squib?"

Bart looked annoyed. "It's a short article."

"Oh. Why didn't you just say that?"

"Because 'squib' sounds better."

Steve had to admit "squib" had a ring to it.

"Anyway, I tried to steal it. You foiled me. And when you wrote me and told me you were keeping the diamond, I saw my chance to get it back. So I wrote you that letter."

"And when my crime lab was vandalized—you were looking for the diamond."

"Yes," said Bart. "The plan was to kidnap you that first day at the hotel. Then you would meet me, we would escape together, I would earn your trust, and you would tell me where the diamond was. But you proved harder to capture than I thought."

Steve smiled briefly, then stopped.

"But your guys tried to kill us at the hotel!" Dana said. "They shot at us. How could Steve tell you where the diamond was if he was dead?"

"They weren't shooting at Steve. They were shooting at you, Dana."

Dana's face flushed.

"Don't feel bad," said Bart. "I'll get rid of both of you once Steve gives me the diamond."

"So that's it?" Dana said. "You're going to kill a couple of kids? You *are* a coward!"

Bart looked up and stared and Dana with his one eye. "But you two don't want to be treated like kids. You want to be treated like detectives."

"That's just Steve," Dana said. "I want to be a veterinarian."

MacArthur Bart ignored him. "And detectives always seek the truth. And the truth is, if the world were fair and good and safe for innocent men, women, and children, then there wouldn't be any need for detectives. But enough," said Bart, jabbing the gun in Steve's face. "Hand over the diamond."

"Why should he, if you're just going to kill us?" Dana said.

Bart sounded impatient. "Because if he gives me the diamond, I'll leave your families alone."

Steve reached into his backpack and pulled out the *Guinness Book of World Records*.

Bart looked confused. "Your secret book-box? We looked in there."

Steve said nothing. He opened the box and pulled out his detective's notebook. He undid the elastic band that held it shut and flipped to the back. There was a tiny secret compartment in the notebook, too.

Steve handed the notebook to Bart. "Here's the diamond," he said. "Although if you were any good, you would have found it yourself."

Bart didn't seem to hear Steve. He was mesmerized. "The Nichols Diamond," he said, holding it up to his eye. It gleamed red and pale in the moonlight. "It's beautiful," said Bart. Bart was about to say something else, but Steve punched him in the solar plexus.

CHAPTER XLVI

THROUGH THE FOREST

BART DOUBLED OVER and held his stomach with both hands. Dana dove for the ground.

"He dropped the diamond!" Dana said. Steve looked over at Bart. He'd also dropped the gun.

Bart fell to his knees and started feeling frantically around in the dirt. Dana was crawling around too.

"Leave the diamond!" Steve said. "Run!"

Steve and Dana took off through the trees.

"Bart said the road was this way," Steve said, huffing as he ran.

"Do you think he was telling the truth?" Dana asked between breaths.

"Why would he lie?" Steve said. "He was still trying to earn our trust."

Branches cracked beneath their feet as they sped along the forest floor.

"What's that?" Dana said. "Up ahead."

Through the trees Steve could see flashing lights. The boys kept running and emerged into a clearing. A few hundred yards away, police cars and tan jeeps were parked on the road, their lights flashing. Flares burned orange on the highway.

"This is where we were kidnapped!" Dana said.

"Police!" came a shout across the clearing.

Great. It was Rick.

And Detective Taylor, plus a guy who looked like a park ranger but carried a gun, all running toward them.

Suddenly the field was all motion and noise. Lights flooded the meadow.

Detective Taylor was leading Steve back to a police cruiser and having him sit in the backseat with Dana. The ranger was talking into his radio, and the radio hissed and crackled back. Three ghostwriters—Antrim and the doorman and Henry, too—were lined up on the pavement, evenly spaced, their hands behind their backs. Rick was saying something about needing more handcuffs. Detective Taylor was reading the ghostwriters their rights, like cops on TV.

There were more rangers, and two policemen in tall black boots. And then came men and women with flashlights and yellow-lettered parkas carrying boxes and plastic bags. "This is unbelievable," Steve heard one say.

"It's like Christmas," said another.

Detective Taylor brought over some granola bars, which Steve and Dana ate eagerly. She crouched down next to them.

"How'd you find us?" asked Dana.

"Park police found Rick's truck hidden by a gray sedan, over behind a rock not too far away."

"Told you there wasn't a secret road," Dana said.

Detective Taylor continued, "We searched the area, and I found a hidden path with fresh footprints that led down to this cave."

"A secret road!" said Steve.

"She said 'hidden path,'" said Dana.

"Anyway," said Detective Taylor, "you guys were right. This Antrim guy wasn't running a literary organization at all—he just confessed to masterminding a crime ring. And those ghostwriters are all part of his gang. You boys did good. What I want to know is how you knew there was something going on with the B. Syndicate."

Steve knew if he told her everything he'd just learned about MacArthur Bart, she wouldn't believe him. Some cases were for the police, and some were for private detectives.

"A hunch," Steve said.

Another car pulled up. A door opened, and then Steve's mom and Dana's parents were there, and they screamed when they saw the boys. Steve and Dana were overwhelmed by hugs and questions.

"I'm so happy you're all right," said Steve's mom.

Steve smiled. "I thought you'd be mad and I'd be in huge trouble."

"I am, and you are," said Steve's mom, and hugged him again. She was crying.

Somewhere, behind them, in the forest, MacArthur Bart was free. But Steve didn't turn around. The moon was disappearing, and the ocean was faintly glowing.

CHAPTER XLVII

CASE CLOSED

STEVE BRIXTON was probably the only private detective in the history of the United States to be personally thanked by the mayor of San Francisco and get grounded by his mother at the same time. Now it was four in the morning, and Steve and Dana were up in Steve's room in Ocean Park. Their parents were downstairs, having a serious conversation in quiet tones.

Steve sat on his bed. Dana sat on his floor. This was probably the last time they'd be spending together outside of school for a while.

"That's it," Steve said. "I retire."

"Seriously?" Dana asked.

"Yes, seriously. Everything I know about being a detective is from a bunch of books written by a criminal."

"But he wrote those books before he went bad," Dana said.

Steve shook his head. "Anyway, when did you start caring about sleuthing?"

"I don't," said Dana. "It just sucks that Bart probably got away with the diamond."

"He didn't," said Steve.

"Yeah, maybe not. He does only have one eye. We should go back up to that forest and look for it. I bet I could find the spot."

Steve smiled. "No, he never got the diamond. That was a Jolly Rancher."

Dana rolled over onto his back and stared up at Steve. "What?"

"Yep. I figured it all out before Bart pulled the gun on us, while we were running up that tunnel in the cave."

"How?"

"You know I do my best thinking on the move."

Dana rolled his eyes. "But how did you figure it out?"

"Handwriting analysis. It's a classic detective's

tool." Steve pulled the threatening note out of his typewriter. "See these *t*'s? They're the same *t*'s as the ones on the ghostwriters' tattoos. I noticed that in the cave. And the whole time we were running, I was wondering who could have written this note and tattooed the ghostwriters. It couldn't have been Antrim. His note in my book had a different *t*. And then I had a hunch. Bart. I didn't want it to be true. But I had to know. So before I pulled out *The Treasure on the Chinese Junk*, I unwrapped a Jolly Rancher and hid it in my notebook. When I saw Bart's inscription, I knew my suspicions were right. So I told him I had the diamond."

"Why?"

"To bring things to a head. Villains never think clearly when there's loot around."

Dana was shaking his head. Steve smiled triumphantly. All this talk of candy was making him hungry. He pulled a Jolly Rancher out of his backpack.

"That's amazing," Dana said. He was sitting up straight now. "Wait—where were you hiding the actual diamond?"

"Oh, I wrapped it up in a another Jolly Rancher wrapper."

"Nice!" Dana mulled that over, then suddenly went ashen. "Steve. If you wrapped up the diamond as a

Jolly Rancher, then there's a chance you unwrapped the actual diamond and gave it back to Bart."

Dana was right. It was possible.

Steve spit. The candy landed on the floor.

"Cherry?" Dana asked.

"Diamond," said Steve.

"Ace!" said Dana.

Steve rolled over and looked at the ceiling. *That's it,* he thought. *I'm done. I'll never solve another case.*

But Steve would solve another case, and soon, and that case would be called *It Happened on a Train.*

Will Steve get drawn back in
to the detective game?
Take a sneak peek at
It Happened on a Train.

THE END

IT WAS WEDNESDAY EVENING, a.k.a. trash night. Steve Brixton, seventh grader, formerly of the Brixton Brothers Detective Agency, plodded along his driveway, dragging a maroon bin behind him. The bin's wheels rumbled and popped as they rolled over pebbles on the blacktop. This week the Brixton family's bin was very full. The lid would not close tightly; it bounced up and down, making an irregular, slow clapping sound. And the trash was heavy—Steve could feel the can's weight in his elbow, and he kept switching the arm he used to drag it: right, then left, and back again. He sighed. Tonight was a particularly difficult trash night, and that's because the garbage bin contained fifty-nine shiny, red-backed books: a complete set of the Bailey Brothers Mysteries, a series of detective novels that until a week and a half ago had been Steve's favorite books of all time.

Steve pulled the bin down off the curb. It hit the street hard, and its lid bounced open like a clam's shell, revealing the can's contents. Steve stood underneath a streetlamp. Its orange bulb flickered and hummed, even though the sun was just now setting and there was still plenty of light in the sky.

There they were, neatly stacked in a cardboard box atop a week's worth of kitchen scraps and dental floss: Bailey Brothers #1 to #58, and of course *The Bailey Brothers' Detective Handbook*, which was jam-packed with Shawn and Kevin Bailey's Real Crime-Solving Tips and Tricks. (Shawn and Kevin Bailey, as pretty much everybody knows, were the sons of world-famous detective Harris Bailey and the heroes of the Bailey Brothers books—they had their own crime lab and fixed their own cars and were basically the acest sleuths around.) The handbook had chapters full of things every serious gumshoe would need to know: stuff like "Tailing Baddies," "Making Your Own Blowgun," and "*Modus Operandi, Portrait Parlé*, and Other Funny Foreign Phrases for the American Sleuth."

Steve stood and stared at his books. He looked around. Identical maroon bins stood like sentries outside every home on the street. The neighborhood was quiet. Assured that he was alone, Steve reached out and picked up a book: Bailey Brothers #15: *The Phantom of Liar's Bluff*, which started like this:

A MYSTERIOUS SIGHTING

"Dad sure is busy with his new case," mused fair-haired Kevin Bailey as he piloted their sedan along the twists and turns of Bayside Road.

"I wonder if he'll let us help out with the sleuthing when he gets back from the Yukon," wondered his younger brother, Shawn, who had dark hair and was a better football player but slightly less handsome.

"Say, fellows, all this talk of work is making me hungry!" whined the

Baileys' stout chum Ernest Plumly, as he nibbled on a hoagie in the backseat.

"I would change the subject," needled Kevin, "but I'm having trouble thinking of a subject that *doesn't* make you hungry."

Shawn and Kevin broke into hearty, good-natured laughter. Ernest, who was almost as well known for his voracious appetite as he was for his loyalty to the Baileys, grinned ruefully. "You fellows can kid me all you want. It's all right. I've got this sandwich to keep me company. I call it the Ernest: shredded lettuce, chopped pickles, smoked ham, roast beef, tomatoes, horseradish, and the secret ingredient: five kinds of mustard."

"Just try not to get any crumbs on the upholstery," joked Kevin. He floored the accelerator, and the sedan tore around a blind curve. The boys spent much of their spare time souping up their Tucker Torpedo, and it was the finest car in Benson Bay. The roar of its engine belied the boys' affectionate nickname for the car: the Jalopy.

The car rounded another curve, and

the Baileys' boathouse appeared.

"There are the girls!" shouted Kevin. "Lay on the horn, why don't you!"

Cissie Merritt and Hannah Fenway waved excitedly when they heard the Jalopy's horn. Kevin often dated pretty, vivacious Cissie. Hannah, Cissie's quiet and doe-eyed best friend, was Shawn's favorite girl in Benson Bay (and the neighboring towns of Kelly Bay and Bayshore, too). The girls were both dressed in bathing suits and carried picnic baskets under their arms, ready for a day aboard the Baileys' speedboat, *The Deducer IV*. The first three *Deducer*s had all been spectacularly wrecked in the Baileys' previous crime-solving exploits.

"I'm so glad we're finally getting to

have this picnic," sang Cissie. "Our last day out was interrupted by that case you two cracked." She was referring to the time Shawn and Kevin busted a gang of carnies and criminal clowns and learned *The Secret Behind the Fun House Mirror.*

"Thanks for not being sore at having to reschedule," offered Shawn, unpacking the trunk. "We'll make it up to you gals on the water. Kevin may be a leadfoot behind the Jalopy, but wait till you see the tricks I can get up to in *The Deducer.*"

The youths laughed together.

"I'm just excited to try out my new present from my dad," beamed Ernest. Mr. Plumly was a prominent lawyer in Benson Bay.

"What did he give you?" asked Shawn.

"I'll give you two sleuths a hint. They're perfect for bird watching."

Ernest pulled a pair of high-powered binoculars out of his satchel.

Shawn and Kevin whistled appreciatively. "That sure is a swell pair of glasses," Kevin commented.

Ernest held the binoculars up to his eyes and peered at the cliffs in the distance. "I can see all the way across to Liar's Bluff from here."

"Say, when do we get a turn, Mr. Audubon?" Hannah smiled.

Ernest didn't say anything. He slowly lowered the binoculars, and his friends noticed that his usually ruddy face had gone pale.

"What's the matter, chum?" Kevin queried. "You look like you've seen a ghost."

"I think I just did!"

Steve's reading was interrupted by squealing brakes. A dented silver station wagon had stopped a few feet from his trash bin. A voice Steve had never heard before shouted, "There you are! I've been looking for you."

POINT PANIC

THE DRIVER'S FACE was gradually revealed as the wagon's grimy passenger-side window descended. Steve guessed he was in his late twenties. He had straight black hair and bright red sunglasses, even though it was dusk. A surfboard was tied to the roof of his car.

Steve's old instincts awoke somewhere near his belly.

Who wore sunglasses at this hour? Criminals, that's who. Also guys who tried too hard to look cool.

Steve looked back toward his house. If this guy tried anything funny, Steve could sprint to his front door in eight seconds. The man was probably harmless, but even a retired sleuth needed to be cautious. He took a closer look at the man's face, just in case he needed to give a description to the cops later. There was a streak of gray, weird for a guy that young, running back from his forehead. A sunburn was peeling near his temples, revealing bright pink skin underneath. And on his left cheek, just below the sunglasses, was a small birthmark in the shape of a pentagon.

The Bailey Brothers' Detective Handbook, which was now somewhere in Steve's trash, has some interesting things to say about birthmarks.

Sometimes successful sleuthing requires some amateur dermatology! The Baileys always pay attention to birthmarks. Red, black, or blue, birthmarks are often the key to cracking a case! Remember Bailey Brothers #26: *The Clue of the Rune in the Ruins*, when Shawn and Kevin unmasked a grave robber posing as the archaeologist Dr. David Franks after noticing the impostor lacked Franks's strawberry-shaped birthmark? It was ace! Of course, birthmarks are also a handy way to identify villainous Masters of Disguise, who often forget to conceal them. In fact many famous criminals have had interesting birthmarks! Here are just a few of the Baileys' favorite examples:

AL CAPONE
Right Thigh
Big Island of Hawaii

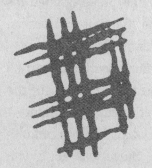

BILLY THE KID
Left Sole
Tartan of the MacDonald
Clan of Lochmaddy

BONNIE PARKER
Right Shoulder
Butterfly, or a Child Crying
Because His Dad
Forgot His Birthday

"Hey," said the man with the pentagonal birth-mark. "Aren't you Steve Brixton?"

"Yeah," said Steve.

The man looked pleased. "Nice! I was coming to see you! You're the famous detective, right?"

Steve shook his head. "I was. Now I'm retired. I just take out the trash for money."

The guy's jaw was slack. His hair hung lankly. "Oh."

After Steve Brixton's first case, *The Case of the Case of Mistaken Identity*, Steve's picture had been in several newspapers. Soon after, Steve opened his own detective agency, just like the Bailey Brothers, and things went terrifically. Until his second case. Steve uncovered *The Ghostwriter Secret* and learned that MacArthur Bart, his hero and the author of the Bailey Brothers books, was a criminal mastermind—who even tried to kill Steve. It was a thrilling but ulti-mately disorienting adventure. Steve was done with private detection. He'd shuttered his agency and started doing chores for ten dollars a week. It wasn't glamorous work, and it paid terribly.

"Why'd you retire?" the man in the car asked.

"It's a long story, but the short version is that nobody likes being lied to."

The man looked confused, probably because there

was no way he could know what Steve was talking about. Still, Steve had liked the way the sentence sounded.

The man brushed his hair out of his eyes, and it fell right back down. "I'm thinking maybe I could convince you to come back and solve one last case?"

"Sorry," said Steve. "I'm out for good."

"I think it's an interesting one."

"Nope."

The man looked at a scrap of paper in his hand. "You worked for the Brixton Brothers Detective Agency, right?"

"Yep."

"So what about your brother? Is he still a detective?"

"I'm an only child."

"Then why is it called—"

"It just sounds cooler, okay?"

"Chill, chill, little man. Look, how much did you charge, you know, back when you were a detective?"

"Two hundred dollars a day, plus expenses."

"I'll double it."

"Nope."

The man in the car seemed disappointed. This was obviously not how he had expected things to go. "Well you can still listen to me, right? I mean, I could tell you about what's going on?"

Steve shrugged. "It's a free country."

The man was encouraged. "Awesome. Okay, Steve—"

"Wait—what's your name?"

"Oh, sorry. I'm Danimal."

"Danimal?"

"Yeah, you know, short for Dan."

"You mean long for Dan."

"What?"

"Never mind."

Danimal was unfazed. "Okay, listen to this. So you know how Mímulo has been closed lately?"

"Yeah," Steve said. "The sharks, right?"

Mímulo Point was a popular surf break about fifteen minutes south of Ocean Park. A few weeks ago a longboarder had spotted a great white shark. More fins had been spotted since, and the area was closed to surfing and swimming. The local news shows had started calling Mímulo "Point Panic."

"Yeah. Sharks. It's brutal, 'cause Mímulo's my favorite spot."

Steve nodded. "Okay."

"But here's the thing—the thing is, I'm not actually scared of sharks. I mean, I wasn't. Because they don't really attack humans, right? I mean, I've got a buddy, a really smart guy, and he's always saying, 'Sharks don't attack humans unless they think they're seals,' right?"

"Sure," said Steve. Steve hated fish. And sharks were the worst fish. Fish eyes never changed, and looking at a fish—whether that fish was swimming in the Ocean Park Aquarium or lying on a bed of ice at some fancy buffet table—made you feel like you didn't exist. But a shark—especially a great white—would eat you, even while it refused to acknowledge your existence, gazewise.

"So what I did was, I customized my wet suit with like these green and orange patches on it. Right? So now I don't look like a seal out there, when I'm sitting in the lineup."

"Yep."

"Okay, so last night was a full moon, and I figured nobody'd be watching the beach at night, and plus the swell was super nice, and I wasn't afraid of sharks, and so, well, I paddled out at Mímulo."

"What?"

Danimal was looking at Steve but not really seeing him. His voice softened. "And I was attacked, man. By a great white."

THE
SEARCH

is just the beginning....

MYSTERY. ADVENTURE. HOMEWORK.

ENTER THE WORLD OF DAN GUTMAN.